I0684506

Bound and Submissive
Sexy Stories Collection

VOLUME 25

10 EROTIC SHORT STORIES

NICHOLE ROGUE

Publisher's Note: This is a work of fiction. Names,
characters, places, and incidents are a product of
the author's imagination. Locales and public
names are sometimes used for atmospheric
purposes. Any resemblance to actual people, living
or dead, or to businesses, companies, events,
institutions, or locales is completely coincidental.

Bound and Submissive/ Nichole Rogue. -- 1st ed.
Xplicit Press, an imprint of TLM Media LLC

ISBN-13: 978-1-62327-556-3
ISBN-10: 1-62327-556-3
eISBN: 978-1-62327-606-5

Printed in the United States of America

CONTENTS

1 RAW STABILITY

"**N**o."

Gabby frowned, crossing her arms, with her eyes fixated on her boyfriend Max. "Why not?"

"Why the hell would I go to some shrink?"

"He isn't a shrink! The ad said he brings couples closer together."

"We're close."

"No we aren't, Max! Don't you get that?"

He rolled his eyes. "You're being a drama queen again, Gab."

Gabby pursed her lips and bit her tongue as her eyes began to sting. It was a typical answer from her boyfriend of two years. They had started dating while they were seniors in high school. Now they were approaching their sophomore year of college, and it felt like everything was going wrong.

"I'm just bringing up legitimate issues," she said. "You don't have to be so mean about it."

"You always bring up the same things."

"Maybe that's because nothing ever changes."

"Whatever, Gabby," he said. "I'm not going."

"I'll go by myself," she said, jutting her chin out.

Max raised his eyebrows. "You're going to go see a guy about strengthening our relationship by yourself? That makes a lot of sense."

Gabby stormed out of the dorm room before the tears started to come, slamming the door behind her.

Crying was something Gabby seemed to do a lot lately. She felt like her life was falling to pieces. She and Max did nothing but fight; she was pretty sure he had cheated on her at least once, and school had proven more than she could handle this year - she had the grades to prove it. All she wanted was stability. If this guy in the ad could provide that, she wanted it.

She called and made the appointment for later that evening after her classes. Another C on a test left her a sobbing mess on her way to the appointment.

Gabby pulled up in front of an old stone

building on the outskirts of town. She checked her appearance in the rear view mirror. She wiped the mascara out from under her big brown doe eyes and ran her fingers through her short blonde hair.

She walked up to the heavy wooden door and knocked on it. A young lady answered with a smile.

"How may I help you?" she asked.

"My name is Gabrielle Williams. I have an appointment to see Lorenzo at 6."

"Right this way." She led her into the house. Gabby felt like she stepped back in time. The whole house was decorated like a medieval castle. She had known it was an old castle, but she'd never thought they'd kept up the tradition by keeping it decorated to period inside. It was the most beautiful home she'd ever been in.

"Mr. Manchester will be with you shortly," the girl said. "Have a seat and wait." She walked off.

Gabby sat down and waited. At six on the dot, the girl came back and said, "Come with me."

She led her up a spiral staircase to one of the large towers all the way at the top. While the office she was led into had maintained its medieval culture, there were modern touches, such as the nice mahogany desk with the laptop and the leather couch and chair set.

"Mr. Manchester will be right with you,"

she said. "Have a seat."

"Thank you," Gabby said, sitting down on the couch. She didn't have to wait long. Five minutes later, the door opened and a man walked in, shutting the door behind him. She sat up a little straighter in her seat.

"Gabrielle?" the man asked with his voice deep and holding the touch of some accent Gabby couldn't place. It was sexy and exotic. He wore a dress shirt and black slacks. His blue shirt conformed nicely to his broad shoulders and thick arms. He had a handsome, freshly shaven face that held a nice summer tan. His dark brown hair looked long enough to fall into his deep blue eyes, but he had it nicely groomed and held in place.

"That's me," she said, her throat gone dry.

He extended his hand. "Pleased to meet you. I'm Lorenzo Manchester."

She stood, shaking his hand. "Nice to meet you."

"Have a seat," he said, sitting down beside her.

"I was hoping my boyfriend would come with me," she said as she sat down. "But he wasn't interested. He doesn't think there's anything wrong. He just says that I'm a drama queen."

"Are you?"

"No! It's not like I go looking for drama. I

4

hate my life. I'd be happy if it were different."

"What is it about your life that makes you unhappy?"

"Everything," she said ruefully. "Max – that's my boyfriend – and I fight all the time. School has gotten progressively harder and my grades are awful. I used to be a straight-A student, and now I'm getting Cs left and right."

"Why do you think your grades are suffering so badly?"

"I don't know! My life just feels like it's falling to pieces and nobody cares. I want some stability in my life, and nobody is offering that to me. Sure as hell not Max."

"So you're here because you want stability."

"I wasn't sure if you'd be able to help me without Max. I know you're really a relationship counselor."

"I'm not a relationship counselor," Lorenzo said. "I'm an alternative lifestyle specialist. I strengthen relationships between couples by finding what exactly the problem is and who is causing the problem, and then I make suggestions on how to fix it using alternative lifestyle methods. Sometimes there's nothing I can do for a couple, or they aren't interested in my suggestions. But I can offer other services as well. And if stability is what you're looking for, I can help you there if you're willing to allow me to work with you."

"Absolutely," Gabby said, nodding. "I'll do anything."

A tiny smile tugged at Lorenzo's lips. "Good to know."

"So what do you think will help me?"

"My suggestion is that you need to get rid of the stressors in your life. One of them sounds like your boyfriend."

"As much as I don't want to think about it, I'm starting to think that you're right about Max. He's not good for me."

"You need someone in your life who won't push your problems under the rug; someone who will listen and respond accordingly. I don't believe you're a drama queen, but I believe that you're letting the stress get to you more than you should."

She frowned a little. "I suppose that's true."

"You need to regain focus. You need to learn what loss of control feels like so you can better control your outside life and learn some self-discipline. You need to prioritize and need to be held accountable."

She chewed on her lower lip. "What do you suggest?"

"I suggest that you see me three times a week. I suggest that during those appointments, you will be stripped of all your defenses and left completely helpless and at my mercy. You'll have to trust me. You will lose all control. You will be held accountable for your poor grades and anything else in your life that needs dealt with."

Swallowing hard, Gabby says, "What exactly do you mean by...left completely helpless and at my mercy?"

"You'll be stripped naked, bound, and blindfolded. I will push you to your limits. You'll be held accountable by being punished. You will not always like it. When you do something good, you'll be rewarded. Our relationship will be from here on out that of Sub and Dom in what is referred to as absolute power exchange. I will micro-manage your life until you can do it yourself. We will start this on a basis of three months. If you still need me after that, we'll enter a contract for another three months and so on."

She squirmed in her seat. The tone of Lorenzo's voice, the easy dominance, and the way his eyes bore right into her soul were everything she'd wanted; everything she'd needed. Here was someone who would punish her when she was bad and reward her when she's good. Someone to micro-manage her life sounded like a good idea, albeit a scary one. And the idea of being pushed to her limits made her stomach twinge and her panties wet.

"I'll do it," she said.

7

"Good. Stand up and take off your clothes."

Gabby blinked, frozen. "I'm sorry?"

"I said stand up and take off your clothes. I did not ask you to question me. Do it again and you'll be punished. Do as I say."

She slowly stood and began to unbutton her pants. Lorenzo stood and crossed the room to his desk. "I'll be testing your limits slowly," he said, rounding the desk. "Because of everyone's threshold for pain being different, we use commands to allow both parties to feel more at ease with each other. These are known as safe words. Begging, pleading, screaming, crying, telling me to stop or yelling out no will not make me stop. These are all natural reactions and necessary in a way to complete the cathartic transformation you will feel afterward."

Gabby pulled her socks off one by one, trying to prolong the process as long as possible. She stood there in her panties and bra, staying silent.

"Yellow will signal to me that it's too much for you to handle, but you don't want me to stop completely," he said. "It may take you a while, but eventually you will be able to handle much more. It's supposed to hurt and you're supposed to be pushed. But if it is absolutely beyond you, you will use it. Red means that you want to completely stop and not go on any longer. Do you understand?"

"Yes."

"Yes, sir," he corrected.

"Yes, sir."

"Take the rest off," he said.

Gabby swallowed hard and hesitated, but unsnapped her bra and sat it on top of her pile of clothing. Slipping her fingers into the hem of her panties, she pushed them down and added them to the pile. She stood there in front of him, feeling very vulnerable.

"Come here."

She walked over and stood inches from him. His eyes assessed her. She shivered in the chill of the office and from the way his blue eyes ran up and down her body, taking stock of her.

"This way," he said, walking toward a door, opening and stepping inside. She followed behind him. "Shut the door." She did as she was told. Lorenzo turned on the light. The room was very primitive, with medieval equipment and various torture devices. Shackles, whips, and chains filled Gabby's mind, making the butterflies in her stomach swarm.

Lorenzo turned to face her. "Have you ever been tied up?"

"No, sir."

"Spanked?"

"No, sir."

"Have you ever thought about it?"

Gabby hesitated. "Maybe."

"Maybe is not an answer, Gabrielle. Maybe means that you don't want to give me the answer and that isn't an option. Have you ever thought about it?"

"Yes, sir."

Lorenzo picked up a blindfold and placed it over Gabby's eyes. "I want you to tell me the top three things you are worst at."

"Um...managing money, poor eating habits, and my grades."

"You said you've been getting Cs. How is your GPA?"

"Slipping," she said. "I started the school year with a 3.69. Now I have a 2.62."

He wrapped rope around her wrists. "Why do you think that is?"

"I don't know."

"You said your life is falling apart. What else is going on in your life other than trouble with Max and your grades?"

Gabby racked her brain. "Well...nothing."

"Do you work?"

"No."

"How does it feel?" he asked, touching his hand to her wrists.

Gabby moved her wrists. It was tight and she was bound but comfortable. "Fine, sir."

"Do you party?"

"Some but not a lot."

"Are you trying your absolute hardest at school? Don't lie to me; I'll know."

Gabby thought about that for a moment before answering, "Well...I suppose not."

"Yes or no, Gabrielle."

"No, sir."

"Lift your arms up."

Gabby lifted her arms above her head. She felt him slip something around the rope. Tugging lightly, she discovered she was locked where she was and unable to move. A rush of helplessness flooded her body, and her heart began to pound.

Lorenzo crossed his arms, watching her. By how intense her breathing began to get, he knew she was getting her first sense of loss of control. Her body was nice and tight and firm. He couldn't understand one of her top three being not eating right. But if it was important to her, it was something they would work on.

"We'll work on your money situation," he said, walking around her, his hand touching her waist, making her shudder. "If you can't manage your money yourself, you'll turn everything over to me, and I'll give you a weekly allowance and a budget until you learn how. We'll set up a meal plan for you that you will strictly follow. Any deviation from it will result in punishment. School will become your main focus. You will have a set schedule of studying. You will not be allowed to go out and party unless you have all of your homework done and never the weekend before a test. From here on out, any grade lower than a B will result in punishment. Once you've brought your grades back up, you'll be rewarded. If you follow your meal plan, you'll be rewarded. If you have money left over at the end of the week, you'll be rewarded."

Gabby chewed on her lower lip. As her heart began to calm down, her whole body had taken on a deep warm feeling. There was a relaxing calm that had come over her at Lorenzo's instructions. She had a strong tingly feeling deep down between her legs. He was not only bringing her comfort but also turning her on.

"As for the pushing your limits part..." Lorenzo's palm handed hard on her backside. She gasped softly. The strike to the other cheek was just as hard, and it made her whimper. He slowly and methodically warmed her backside until it was a glowing red, and she was squirming all over and breathing heavily.

"There is a difference between when I'm training you and when I'm punishing you," he added, his hand now softly stroking her bottom, making her sigh. "Right now I'm pushing you. I'm engaging you in something foreign and unknown to you. You're naked in front of a man you just met, bound and blindfolded at his will, and being spanked. You're learning to trust. You're learning loss of control. Only in the loss of control can you truly be in control. Do you understand?"

"Yes, sir."

He patted her rump. "Good girl." He untied her and turned her to face him, pulling the blindfold off. "That's enough for today." He untied her wrists. "Come back tomorrow at the same time, and we'll further discuss the rest of the week and get a formal contract signed. If you choose not to come back tomorrow, that's your choice." He gave her a soft kiss on the lips and said, "Either way, you should dump your boyfriend."

Gabby smiled and said, "Thank you, sir."

Three months later, Gabby was happier than she had been in years. The first thing she'd done when she'd gotten back home was call Max and tell him they were over. The sting of him acting like he didn't care led her to binge eat the entire week. She'd tasted her first real punishment from

Lorenzo from not following the meal plan. It had been the most liberating and cathartic experience of her life. Since then, she'd only been punished three other times – once for getting poor grades on her finals, once for blowing all her money and needing more halfway through the week, and the other for her attitude during one of their sessions.

At the moment, she was nude, ass up across his knee, his hand raining down across her rear. It wasn't as punishment; it was part of her training. She'd learned early on that when she was punished; it was with an implement. It was colder and harsher with no contact. It made her know that she'd done wrong. When he trained her, as he pushed her limits to cleanse her, he used his hand. It was much more intimate. It turned her on and made her want him. She needed every ounce of their relationship, but this was the part she got the most gratification out of.

Lorenzo paused, rubbing his hand across her raw ass. Her breaths were coming out in short shudders. "Where are you at, Gabrielle?"

"Still green, sir," she replied breathlessly. She longed for more. It was a sexual experience for her. Even if he pushed her so far she cried, it made her feel closer to him.

He studied her ass and patted it.

"You've had enough for now. Stand up."

She stood and placed her wrists behind her back as she'd been instructed to earlier.

"Today is the end of our contract," he said. "You've done well. Your grades have come up an entire grade point since last semester, you're managing your money much better, and you haven't deviated away from your meal plan in two months."

"Yes, sir. I know."

Lorenzo brushed some hair out of her face. "You have enough self-discipline now to manage your own life, if you choose to."

Gabby rolled her lips, her eyes betraying everything her mouth wasn't saying.

"Gabrielle?" he asked, his blue eyes looking deep into her brown ones. "Speak."

"I don't want our contract to expire," she said. "I feel so much more confident and in control of myself with you around."

He touched her hair again, his fingers running through the silky blond strands. "I don't think we should renew our contract."

She felt hurt, but simply said, "Oh."

"Because now that it's expired, I feel comfortable doing this." He pulled her closer, leaning down and enclosing his mouth around hers. She melted into him, wrapping her arms around his neck. They were still there as he pulled back.

"Do you do this with all your clients?"

He tugged her hair to the side, so she was looking into his eye. His hand crashed down against her rear disapprovingly and she gasped. "Never," he said. "There's just something about you...I can't put my finger on."

Gabby bit her lower lip. "I've been wanting you to kiss me for months now."

"I know," he said, smirking a bit. "We don't have to change much, you know. For the most part, things will remain the same, with more sexuality..." His hands skimmed up her rib cage to her breasts; his thumbs brushing across her erect nipples. "...brought into the mix. I can take you to a whole other level of submission if you aren't my client."

The thought sent a thrill through Gabby's body. "So what would I be, sir?"

"You'd be my Sub...and preferably, my girlfriend."

"I like that idea."

He tugged her closer, crushing his mouth down on hers. She whimpered as his hands wandered down the length of her, exploring the body he had come to know so well. His mouth moved to her neck, her chest, and to her breasts. His teeth and tongue assaulted her nipples until she was moaning loudly; her face buried in his chest, her knees buckling.

"So you want me?" he whispered in her

ear, nibbling on the lobe.

"Oh God...yes, sir."

He pushed her down onto the couch, kissing down her body, his tongue leaving a trail down her belly that made her shudder. He nibbled the inside of her thigh, nipping at the sensitive flesh. Gabby gasped, her hand clutching at the cushion. Lorenzo pulled his polo shirt over his head and took his slacks off. His erection brushed across Gabby's belly as he leaned over to kiss her. He pulled his boxers off and spread her legs. The tip of him teased at her wet opening. He pushed her wrists above her head, holding them in place with a hand as he slid inside her. She closed her eyes, gasping, feeling every inch of him as he went deep in until she touched the base of him. He thrust hard, making her gasp and moan with each one, his fingers digging into her wrists.

"Open your eyes," he said. She did so, locking hers onto his. His fingers rolled her nipples, squeezing, tugging, playing, and making little electric shocks shoot through her body. She thrashed about underneath him - squealing, moaning, and gasping with each shudder that came over her.

"Oh my God..." She gasped, her muscles tensing. "I'm gonna cum..."

He thrust harder, deeper, saying, "Do it."

Her body rose up off the couch, the scream ripping out of her throat, echoing off the walls. Lorenzo grasped her around her arched waist, grunting with each hard movement through her tightening walls.

"Oh God, sir! Ooh!" She moaned. He groaned above her, and she felt his warmth flood inside her.

He leaned down to kiss her. She kept her arms where he had placed them. He smiled at her. "Good girl," he said with a tiny grin.

Gabby just smiled, never more content with her life than at that moment.

Continued in Raw Submission.

2 RAW SUBMISSION
Raw Stability 2

Gabby's legs shook with exertion, and the muscles in her arms ached. The ¾ of a way full glass of water she balanced on her head sloshed a bit as her body jerked. She was naked, bent over, holding her body in position, and her arms holding the glass of water up right on her head. Her boyfriend and top Lorenzo was running a feather up and down her thighs. Every muscle in her body tightened as the feather brushed against her wet pussy and across her red ass.

"Don't spill it," his voice commanded. "You know what happens if you do."

She did know – because she had done it twice already. The red lashes across her back, rear, and thighs still burned. This had been going on for an hour now. He had told her it was a test of self-control. She was apparently failing it miserably.

Lorenzo slid a finger inside her and she gasped, dropping the glass. She cringed as it shattered against the concrete floor.

"Gabrielle..." he said firmly.

"Sorry, sir." She gasped as the whip sliced across her already sore backside. She bit her lip as the delicious burn sunk deep in, sending waves of pain and pleasure through her core. The crack of it through the air made her shiver, and the pain of it made her cry out. The sting brought tears to her eyes, making her whimper.

"Obviously, you need some more training before you're capable of this lesson," Lorenzo said, lashing the whip across her backside a final time. "Stand up and face me with your hands behind your head."

Gabby did as she was told, lacing her fingers behind her head and turning to face her master. "I'm sorry I disappointed you, sir."

"We'll try again next week. Maybe if I use the paddle on you instead, it will sink in better."

"Yes, sir."

He squeezed a nipple between his fingers, making her bite her lip, the pain enveloping her in bliss. "I don't think you'll be getting any release today, Gabrielle."

"Oh, please, sir…"

"No. That's your punishment for disappointing me."

She frowned.

"And if I catch you masturbating…"

"You won't, sir. May I pleasure you, sir?"

"No," he said. "You enjoy it too much. I'll take care of myself. In fact…" He took a step back and unbuttoned his pants. He pulled his dick out and began to rub his hand up and down it. The flutter of his eyes and the soft groans escaping his throat made Gabby hot. Her stomach ached and her pussy trembled, desperately wanting to touch him and to be touched. He stepped closer, his eyes locking on hers, darkening as he jerked his hand harder. He groaned deeply as he came, his warm seed gushing out against her belly.

"Go get cleaned up, pet," he said, kissing her softly, rubbing her rump.

She leaned into his touch, melting. "Yes, sir."

Gabby couldn't remember a time that she'd ever been so calm, relaxed, and at peace with her life. When she'd first met Lorenzo, she'd never expected him to encompass her life in such a positive way. She loved him and worshipped him in every sense of the word. They'd been together for a month but known each other for four. He could bring her to new heights of pain and pleasure that she'd never experienced in her life. He pushed her beyond her limits, and she'd found she loved every moment of it. At one point in time, she'd felt her whole life was spinning of control. Now everything made sense. She'd never felt so fulfilled, even when forced to be unfulfilled.

It was the weekend and it was theirs. Both days they remained at play from sun up to sun down. She relished those days. It made her Mondays so much better, and she felt a glow about her the entire week later.

Gabby watched as Lorenzo tightened the leather shackles around her wrists. She was lying on her back on a bench and her arms stretched out above her head with her wrists secured. Her legs were up in the air, her ankles shackled to a suspension bar, leaving her spread eagle, and elevated up off the bench a few inches. He placed a blindfold over her eyes, and within moments she felt her other senses heighten. She could hear his foot falls as he crossed the room, gathering whatever instruments he would be using on her. They'd discussed at length when first getting together what she would try, might try, and wouldn't try. Everything on her would try list was free game during their weekend play sessions. He never told her ahead of time what would be happening, and she liked it that way. She loved the anxious feeling of butterflies swarming in her belly as she waited to find out what we would do.

"Comfortable?" he asked.

"Yes, sir."

He flicked at a nipple and it instantly hardened. He squeezed it and then she felt the cold metal pressure of the clamp squeezing down, gripping the tender flesh. She whimpered softly as the waves of pleasure shot through her once and then twice as he placed the clamp on the opposite one. "Still?" he asked.

"Yes, sir…"

His hand slid up her belly, between her breasts, to her neck. He kissed her softly, his hand applying gentle pressure, making her hearing dull and her heart pound in her chest. He pulled his hand away as the kiss stopped. She gasped softly, breathing in deeply, letting the oxygen seep through her pores and her heart to stop pounding. She heard his shoes against the concrete as he circled around her. The sting of the crop against her thigh made her gasp and her body buck. Her body jerked with each crack up and down her thigh and across her backside, back up the other thigh. The delectable pain encircled her, drowning her, pulling her down into a deep hole of pleasure until she felt as though her body were floating. The echoes of the leather against skin sounded miles away to her. She felt nothing but a deep, overwhelming calm.

After what felt like ages, she began to slowly accept reality back. She could feel her top's hand caressing her backside. The pressure of the clamps came back next and then the intense burning of the flesh on her ass and thighs.

"That was lovely," she said breathlessly. She whimpered softly as Lorenzo's fingers slid inside her. "Oh, god...sir..."

"Cum, pet," he said, his fingers stroking her, bringing her to the brink, making her body shudder and the walls of her pussy tighten around them. "Good girl..." He kissed her inner thigh, pulling his fingers out. "Are you tired?"

"Yes, sir..."

"I'm going to leave you here for a while, alright? Sleep if you need to."

"Thank you, sir..." She rested her head to the side and quickly fell asleep.

క్రుడ

The sounds of Lorenzo milling about their dungeon stirred Gabby. She had a momentary second of panic at her lack of sight but then remembered her blindfold.

The clamps had been removed from her nipples. Her backside still ached from earlier.

"Are you awake, pet?" he asked.

"Yes, sir." She gasped at the feeling of the white-hot feeling of ice against her tender nipples. She whimpered as he rubbed the corner around in circles against both nipples, leaving them hard and swollen. The cold water dripped down her belly as the ice melted in his hand. When the ice touched the raw flesh of her thighs and ass, she sighed at how good it felt. He brushed the ice against the pussy and she moaned. He rubbed it across her clit and she bit her lip, shuddering. He leaned over, blowing on her nipples, causing shivers to run down her spine.

"How are you feeling?" he asked.

"Good, sir."

His tongue ran in circles around her cold nipples. A deep groan gurgled from her lips. She loved the feeling of his tongue against her body. He could make her scream with a few simple strokes against her pussy with a velvety thing. It was a rare treat and she reveled in it when she got it.

"You've been a very good girl lately," he told her.

"I disappointed you yesterday, sir."

"We'll work on it next weekend. But you've been doing very well with money and in school. Everything has improved dramatically. You haven't been punished in quite some time."

Gabby moaned as he licked his way across her belly, his warm tongue trailing a line of cold water. "Yes, sir...I've been trying."

"How do you think your grades will be for midterms?"

"Good, sir."

"You won't need punished?"

"No, sir."

"If I reward you, will I regret it later this week?"

"No, sir," she promised.

He dipped his head between her legs, his tongue flicking across her clit. She whimpered, her teeth catching her lower lip, her body jerking with the powerful surge of pleasure.

"You'd better be right, Gabrielle."

"I am, sir...ooh god...I swear." Her back arched up as his tongue lapped at her, shooting liquid fire through her veins. "Oh, sir...oh...!"

"You can cum, pet."

She tugged on her shackles, screaming his name as the orgasm ripped through her body, leaving her spent. Lorenzo patted her rump and said, "Good girl."

Gabby had been right about her grades. She'd received high marks in everything, pulling nearly a 4.0. What she hadn't been counting on was the speeding ticket she would get on her way home that Wednesday.

Her eyes followed Lorenzo as he paced back and forth slowly, reading the ticket. "This is going to be a lot of money, Gabrielle."

"I know, sir."

"This isn't the first speeding ticket you've gotten. I let the other one pass because everyone makes mistakes. But because this is the second one in a month, you need to be taught a lesson."

"Yes, sir."

"It's been a while since you've been punished, Gabrielle. I want you to go downstairs, remove all your clothing, and kneel against the wall with your hands behind your back. I'll be there shortly."

"Yes, sir," she said, walking off toward the basement. Her stomach swarmed with butterflies. She'd only been punished five times outside of play. When they were playing a scene, the discipline she incurred was sexual and turned her on. He pushed her to the edge of pain and pleasure, pulling back enough to send her into a deep euphoria. A punishment was meant to teach her a lesson and alter her behavior. And while it was a cathartic and cleansing experience, she never looked forward to them eagerly.

Gabby stripped off her clothes and sat them on top of a sawhorse. She knelt onto the concrete and laced her hands behind her back, waiting for her disciplinarian.

"Stand up, Gabrielle," Lorenzo said firmly from behind her. She did as she was told. "Face me." She turned around, her eyes to the floor. "Look at me." She met his disappointed eyes. "We're going to take care of this today and then move on. The ticket will be paid, and it won't happen again."

"Understood, sir."

"Turn around and bend over, placing your hands flat against the wall."

Gabby turned and bent over, stretching her back out, laying her hands against the wall. Out of the corner of her eye, she saw Lorenzo choose a cane from the rack. Her stomach tumbled to her feet. She hated the cane. He'd used it on her once when she'd disobeyed him, and it had been worse than the whip.

"You went ten miles over the speed limit," he said. "You'll receive ten for each mile and two to make you think about what you've done. Then you're to go straight up to bed. Are we clear?"

"Yes, sir."

The evil implement tapped at her exposed backside. The swish through the air made her squeeze her eyes shut, anticipating the biting pain that occurred two seconds later. The line lit on fire across her ass, sending a shock of agony through her system that made her gasp softly. The second one landed just below it and the third below that. The fifth landed on the crease between her cheek and thigh, making her bounce up and down on the balls of her feet, whimpering softly.

"Stay still," he commanded.

"Yes, sir," she said breathlessly. Her whole backside was on fire, each welting stripe causing a deep sting that made her eyes water. By the last one, there were tears streaming down her face, her breathing ragged and heavy. Lorenzo's hand rested against the battered flesh, the coolness of it making her sigh softly.

"Have you learned a lesson, pet?"

"Yes, sir," she responded softly.

"Stand up and face me."

She did so. He reached out and wiped away her tears. "All is forgiven." He took her face in his hands and kissed her softly. "Go up to bed now."

"Yes, sir." She walked upstairs toward their bedroom, sniffling, rubbing her sore backside. She felt calm and purified. Through the throbbing pain, she just felt such a connection with her lover that she wanted him in her arms. She lay in bed on her side, her hand stroking across the raised marks on her backside, longing to have Lorenzo in bed with her. She thought this was further punishment – no love, hugs, or kisses aside from the one to prove she was forgiven.

Her back was turned to the door when he entered. He slipped into bed beside her, wrapping his arms around her waist.

"I thought you were punishing me further by sleeping in the guest room," she said.

"Never, Gabrielle," he said, kissing the back of her neck softly. "You've been punished enough." His gentle hand caressed her punished skin, his lips touching her shoulder. "You know I love you too much to do that."

She sighed softly as his hand stroked her hips and across her belly, up to cup her breast. His mouth touched her shoulder and neck and his tongue grazing her ear lobe. "Sweet Gabrielle," he whispered in her ear as his thumb gently stroked her nipple, making her sigh and shiver. "Such a beautiful young lady." He rolled her over to face him, gathering her into his arms, his hands touching her, making her lips part. He leaned in, kissing her softly. His teeth nibbled on her lower lip and his fingers caressing her wetness slowly, warming her body, making a soft simmer grow inside her. "Do you love me, pet?"

"Oh, yes, sir," she responded, closing her eyes, soaking in the feeling of his long fingers stroking her. "So very much."

He pulled her to him, slipping his erection between her legs. He kissed her, rolling her onto her back, spreading her legs. As he entered her slowly, she whimpered into his mouth, her back arching and her pussy involuntarily tightening. "Look at me," he said softly into her ear, kissing her neck. She opened her eyes to look up into his. He moved slowly, firmly, thrusting deep but gentle as he took her, pulling her down as deep as he had with the crop, dragging her into a euphoria so far down she couldn't even make a sound as it enveloped her, tightening her around him, sending trembling waves throughout her body, and making his name shudder from her lips softly as he brought her crashing over each ebb and flow until she was spent and exhausted.

Lorenzo wrapped her close to him, kissing her, staying inside her as he rolled to the side, and his strong arms holding her tight. She felt him fall limp inside her after he came. The feeling of him still inside her made her feel warm and content. He kissed her forehead, brushing her hair out of her face.

"Good girl, Gabrielle," he said softly, kissing her again. "Good girl."

She smiled, resting her head against his chest. "Thank you, sir."

3 WRONG SIDE OF THE WHIP

Zooey jogged down the sidewalk toward Gamma Beta Tau, rushing past some of her sisters on the lawn. She ran into the house and toward the stairs.

"Where's the fire?" Carrie, the sorority president, asked her.

"I'm heading to see Archer."

Carrie turned up her nose. "Why are you still with him? He's not of your caliber."

"Because I like him?" Zooey responded in a sarcastic tone.

"He is pretty hot," Jenna, the vice-president, said.

"He's a biker," Carrie said in disgust. "And he's part of Alpha Delta Pi, so that automatically puts him off limits."

"Oh well!" Zooey ran upstairs into her room. She started searching through her closet. Her sisters didn't understand and they couldn't. Her and Archer's relationship was not like other relationships. She changed into a pleated black skirt and grabbed a white blouse, putting it on and tying it in the front, buttoning it up enough to be halfway modest. Her sisters all thought she was trying to be a trendsetter with the way that she dressed, but that wasn't the case at all. Zooey parted her brown hair in the back and put pigtails in and finally she pulled on a pair of white knee-high socks and slipped into some black shoes and she was out the door again.

"You look cute!" Jenna said.

"Thanks!" She ran out the door and headed toward Alpha Delta Pi.

Gamma Beta Tau was the top sorority on campus. The good girls got into Gamma Beta. They were the overachievers, the ones who placed grades before partying. Gamma Beta's sisters were known for their poise, their charity work, their academics, and their athletics. They networked with the best fraternities on campus—and Alpha Delta wasn't it.

Alpha Delta was the laughing stock of the Greek community. They were the animal house of the university. They threw parties three times a week and had the worst cumulative grade point average on campus. Zooey's boyfriend Archer was president of the laughing stock. They were, to say the least, a controversial couple on campus.

Zooey walked into the fraternity house. The guys sitting around the living room whooped and hollered, whistling cat calls at her as she walked through.

"Quiet!" Archer said, standing, giving them all a head shake. "Really, boys. Where are your manners?" He rested his hands on her hips, looking her up and down. He met her eyes, the green in the hazel irises sparkling back at her. "Very nice."

She smiled coyly. "I thought so."

Archer took her hand and headed toward the door to the basement, where his bedroom was. They walked down the steps, and he shut and locked the door behind them.

"I like it," he said. He crossed his arms. "Turn around."

Zooey held out her arms and did a slow turn before stopping back in front of him. Archer had short brown hair he liked to spike with gel. His hazel eyes were hard and icy when he was being commanding, soft, and sensual when he was being sexy. His muscular arms were strong enough to hold her up while he hoisted her against the wall and his tight thighs were a testament to many years straddling a motorcycle.

"I like it a lot," he added, stepping toward her, backing her up against the wall. "Too bad it's going to be coming off in a few minutes." He raised her arms up above her head, pinning them against the cold cement.

"A few, huh?"

He nipped at her neck. "Yep." He bit her ear lobe and she inhaled sharply. "So what should it be today...?" He looked deep into her brown eyes. "I'm thinking I tie you down...torture you...make you beg for mercy...and then just when you can't take anymore...bend you over and fuck your brains out."

Zooey bit her lower lip, saying nothing, her panties already soaking wet. She wanted to lean into him and rub against him, but she knew better, although sometimes she did it so he would react and punish her but that day she wanted to be a good girl.

Archer held her wrists with one hand, his other cupping her braless breast, skimming a thumb across the hard nipple. She gasped. He pinched and tugged, making tiny grunts and whimpers come out of her throat. He took a step back. "Take off your shirt," he commanded.

Zooey untied, unbuttoned, and shrugged the fabric over her shoulders, letting it float to the ground.

"Arms behind your back."

She crossed her arms behind her back, a hand grasping each arm. Archer hooked a finger around the hem of her skirt, pulling her closer. He pinched a nipple between his fingers, saying, "Not a sound. And do not move."

Zooey bit her lip, struggling to stay still and willing herself to stay silent as Archer rolled the sensitive flesh back and forth between his thumb and forefinger. Her stomach quivered and her pussy begged for release as he took her nipple in his free hand. He tugged on them both, and she clenched her teeth and squeezed her eyes shut, struggling, starting to sweat from the effort.

Archer released her and her eyes opened. He patted her hip. "Good girl," he said, running his hands up her ribs. "Very good girl." He pulled her into him, his hand sliding down to cup her ass, his mouth enclosing around hers. She melted into him, her hands still behind her back and her lips parting to let him in. His tongue caressed hers possessively, his teeth gnashing against her lips, tugging playfully and greedily.

Both his hands slid under her skirt pulling her panties down. He parted her legs and slid a finger inside. She sucked in air, mouthing soundlessly as his middle finger brushed across her throbbing clit, liquid fire igniting through her veins.

"Not a sound," he warned.

Zooey practiced breathing to keep from moaning as he massaged her most sensitive part. Her legs shook, feeling weak. As the sweet release ripped through her, she clenched her teeth and let it wash over her in silence, the deep ripple of each wave slamming through her body like a tidal wave. He slipped his finger out and smiled approvingly, patting her rump.

"Good girl," he repeated, kissing her. "You can talk again."

"Oh my God," she said with a gasp.

Archer wrapped his arms around her waist, picking her up and sitting her on his desk. He pulled her shoes off and then her socks, slowly, sensually. Zooey shivered as his cool hands slid up her thighs. He tugged her forward, sliding her across the slick wood surface to the edge. He unbuckled his belt and let his jeans fall. He removed his erection from his boxers and pulled her close, burying himself inside her. Zooey sighed deeply, her head dropping back, drinking in the feeling of him brushing against her.

He tugged her as far to the edge as she could go without falling, thrusting into her roughly. She groaned, longing to touch him and to feel his muscles ripple underneath his flesh, but he hadn't released her. Until he told her she could move her arms, that's where they would stay. She was obedient. She had learned over the year they had been together what was expected of her. It was a fairly simple and very satisfying arrangement. She had found out that she loved being dominated—especially by him.

Archer groaned deeply as Zooey convulsed around his dick, squeezing him tight. His hands gripped her thighs as he shuddered and emptied his warm cream inside her. He grasped her behind the head, pulling her in for a long, passionate kiss that left Zooey whimpering.

"Go get cleaned up," he whispered in her ear. "Then comes the tying you down and torturing you until you beg me for mercy part."

Zooey gnawed on her lip, grinning a little. "Yes, sir," she responded.

Zooey trotted down to the kitchen the next morning. She grabbed an apple out of the basket on the counter.

"Are you excited about our camping trip?" Jenna asked.

"Yes!"

"I'm not," Carrie said disdainfully. "I can't believe we're going with Alpha Delta. What a joke. They're going to make us the laughing stocks."

"Lighten up, Carrie," Jenna said. "Don't go if you don't want to be seen with them."

"Whatever. It's free so why not?"

"Too bad rules require you and Archer to share separate cabins," Jenna said.

"That's disgusting, Jenna," Carrie sneered.

Zooey rolled her eyes and walked off, not wanting to hear it. She and Archer would find a way around the rules. The only rules she cared about were the ones that he set.

Archer's uncle owned the campground they were staying at, and he'd offered to let him and his friends along with another fraternity or sorority of Archer's choosing come up for the weekend free of charge. And that was how the worst fraternity on campus ended up camping out with the best sorority on campus.

"This place is huge," Zooey remarked, looking around in awe.

"It's nice," Archer agreed with a nod. "I've been here a million times, but it's nice."

"It'll do," Carrie said haughtily as she strode by with her pink suitcase.

"I hate her," Archer stated.

Zooey giggled.

He hooked an arm around her waist and pulled her close, kissing her. "Meet me outside by this tree," he said, nodding toward a big oak. "Tonight at eleven."

"Yes, sir," she answered with a grin.

He kissed her and walked off toward his half of the campground.

Zooey headed to her cabin and to her room. Having the whole campground to themselves, they were all able to have their own rooms. Zooey laid out all the clothes she had brought. She had brought one whole suitcase filled with just sexy outfits.

She chose a pair of lacy red thongs and chose to go braless again, just the way he preferred. She grabbed a dress and pulled it over her head, adjusting it. It was a black strapless that conformed nicely to her unsupported breasts and fell just below her ass, showing off a little bit of butt cheek and bared it all if she bent over. There were five slashes going up both sides, showing flesh through every single gash in the fabric. She had never worn it for him before. She slipped on some black high heels and waited.

Eleven drew close. Zooey knew not to be late. She snuck out without an issue, all the other girls having gone to bed. She leaned against the tree and waited. Archer wasn't a moment sooner or later.

His eyes scanned up and down her body as he approached, carrying a backpack. "You look...positively naughty," he said, tilting his head, his tiny grin showing approval. "When did you get this?"

"Yesterday," she said. "You like?"

"I very much like it. Turn."

She did so, very slowly, allowing him to absorb the look from behind. She even stuck her rear out a little so he could see the flash of her plump bum underneath the fabric.

"You..." He pulled her close. "Are a very, very naughty little girl."

"Only for you."

He kissed her hard, shoving her up against the tree. His hands slid down her sides, his teeth biting her lips, her neck, and her chest.

"I brought a little something," he said. "And from your outfit, it's fitting."

"Sounds mysterious."

"It was meant to." He pointed into the woods. "Further in."

"Yes, sir," she said teasingly. She turned and started walking. He landed a playful swat on her rump, following behind.

Zooey and Archer wandered deep inside the woods until they were far away from the cabins. There was dim light from the moon and the trees cast shadows everywhere Zooey looked.

"I'm going to tie you up," Archer stated.

Zooey's heart skipped a beat and her belly shivered. "I think you also need a good spanking, but we'll save that for tomorrow." His hands fell to his belt buckle. "Down on your knees."

Zooey eagerly knelt in front of him, her knees digging into the soft grass.

"Hands behind your back."

She obeyed him. She watched as he unzipped his pants and pulled out his dick. He grasped her behind the head and stepped closer, drawing her into him. She opened her mouth and allowed him to place his half-mast member in her mouth. She closed her eyes, savoring the feeling of his skin sliding across her lips, the sweet feeling of the rush of blood entering him as he grew against her tongue. She slid her head back as far as he would let her, his fingers tangled in her hair, binding her tightly. He thrust inside her, to the back of her throat. She took him in, twisting her head slightly, making small groans gurgle from deep inside his chest.

The wetness between Zooey's legs was seeping out against the lacy fabric. She longed to have him touch her. The idea of being tied up and fucked by him in the woods sent a thrill through her. He yanked her back and up to her feet.

"Back against the tree," he told her firmly. She did as she was told. He pulled a rope out of his backpack. He pulled her arms back around on either side of the tree. The bark scraped against her skin as he did. The rope burned as he tied it around each wrist and tugged it tight, tying it behind the tree. She couldn't move. She was helpless and at his total will. A shiver went down her spine.

Archer tugged the top of her dress down, exposing her breasts. He tweaked each one, saying, "You don't have to be quiet. Make as many sounds as you want. You may need to."

He dipped his head down, taking a tight, cold nipple into his mouth and sucking. She gasped. He bit, grazing his teeth against the sensitive skin. She squirmed, whimpering, gasping, squealing as he tortured her breasts each one slowly in turn before going back to the other one. She was panting out short sobs of pleasure, begging, "Oh God, please...just fuck me..."

"I will fuck you when I'm good and ready," he said firmly. "Don't make me untie you and spank you tonight."

"Yes, sir."

Archer pulled a vibrator out of the bag. The buzz sounded loud in the quiet woods, the only other sound the chirping of crickets. When he touched it to her moist panties, she gritted her teeth and shuddered. He yanked her panties down around her ankles and pulled her dress up, exposing her to the cool air.

"Lift up your legs," he said, stepping closer. "Place them against my hips."

She lifted her legs up. As close as he was, she had to bend her knees, opening herself wide for him, to rest her high heels against his jeans. He touched the vibrator to her clit and she clunked her head back against the trunk of the tree.

"Ooohh..." She moaned, moving her hips forward the best she could, her pussy shuddering with ecstasy through each jolt of pleasure being shot through her.

"That feels good?" he asked, sliding a couple fingers inside her, feeling it tighten around them. "Hmm?" He wiggled them around, making her whimper and whine. He kissed her hard, tossing the vibrator to the ground and dropping his pants. He thrust inside hard, causing her to cry out. He drove into her hard and fast, making her take every inch of him. Her legs shook with the ferocity of each movement, the tree bark scratched at exposed skin, the pain egging her on. He held onto the tree trunk, his eyes locked on hers, as he took her, claiming her, reminding her just who was in charge. She didn't need reminded. She knew. And she loved every minute of it.

"Scream," he told her. "I want you to scream my name. I don't care if they hear you. I want you to come and I want you to scream."

"Oh, God, yes sir," she said, whimpering, her whole body shuddering with the sweet release. Letting go of herself and crying out, the shriek ripped through her body so loud she was sure she woke up the campground. "Oh God! Archer! Oh, don't stop!"

Archer growled, biting her neck, leaving a trail of red marks from her neck down to her breasts, plunging inside her until her legs felt like jelly and her throat was hoarse from screaming. As she moaned with one final, shuddery orgasm, Archer groaned and came inside her.

He took a step back and took a towel out of his bag, wiping himself off. He observed her; she looked spent... He untied her and helped steady her, wrapping his arms around her waist, drawing her into him.

"You know you're mine, don't you?" he whispered in her ear, nuzzling against her hair.

"Yes."

"And you love it."

"More than you'll ever know."

4 FORCING HIS HAND

"We're going on a cruise?" Hannah Martin asked her dad, her blue eyes lighting up with joy. "That's great!" Her smile fell as she turned to look at her parent's friends. "Wait...what did you mean by we all are going?"

"We're all going," Mrs. Martin said. "You, your father and I, and the Chapin's."

Hannah locked eyes with Dominick Chapin. The scowl on his face let her know that he wasn't any happier about it than she was. Neither of them had been able to stand the other since the day they had met as twelve year olds.

"We'll be going to the island," Mr. Martin said, referring to the small semi-private island that he co-owned with business associates. "We will have the entire east side all to ourselves."

"That sounds amazing," Mrs. Chapin said. "I don't even know how to thank you for inviting us along."

"It's a once in a lifetime opportunity," Mr. Chapin said. He looked at his son and nudged him.

"Thank you," Dominick said. "Really, it's so very generous of you."

Dominick would have been a lot happier about the idea of a cruise and an island paradise if he didn't know he would have to spend a week with Hannah Martin. He had never met anyone as snobby, bratty, and stuck up as Hannah. She had had everything handed to her on a silver platter from the time she was born. While he had to get loans and bust his ass to afford the private university that they went to all Hannah had to do was call up her daddy and ask for a loan and he'd deposit money into her checking account. He liked and respected Mister and Mrs. Martin, but he despised their spoiled daughter.

"When do we leave?" Hannah asked.

"Tomorrow morning," Mr. Martin said. "Get packed up and ready to go!"

"I can't be ready tomorrow! I don't have a bathing suit!"

"You have tons of bathing suits, honey," Mrs. Martin said.

"From last year," she said with a sneer.

"Ugh."

Dominick snorted. His father elbowed him and he shut up.

"We'll go shopping today," Mrs. Martin conceded.

She grinned. "Great!"

Dominick shook his head. It was going to be a long week.

Hannah leaned over the railing of the cruise ship, closing her eyes and letting the wind whip her hair around behind her. The hot sun beat down on her bare shoulders and legs. The spray of the ocean misted her face and cooled her down.

Dominick approached from behind slowly, taking a lengthy look at the young woman's long toned and tan legs and the way her denim short-shorts molded to her backside. Hannah's waist length blonde hair fell just above her rear, billowing in the breeze.

"Hey," he said.

She opened her eyes. "What do you want?"

"It's a free boat," he said, leaning back against the railing, facing the ship. "And I just thought I'd say hi."

"There's an entire ship to wander and you have to stand beside me."

"You don't have to be such a stuck-up

little brat, Hannah," he said. "Seriously."

"You don't have to be such a jerk."

"How am I being a jerk?" he asked. "I was being polite and saying hi. So shoot me." He pushed himself away from the railing, heading over to one of the lounge chairs. He pulled his shirt over his head and lay down, closing his eyes.

Hannah blinked, thankful for the sunglasses covering her eyes. She could not stop herself from staring at Dominick's nicely chiseled chest and well-defined abs. His shoulders and upper arms were ripped with nicely cut muscles. His shaggy brown hair fell down into his face; his sunglasses covered his brown eyes. It was all she could do to keep from drooling until she remembered who she was looking at. Angry with herself for the flush of desire that rocked through her she stomped off.

The cruise to the island took two days. Hannah and Dominick avoided each other as much as possible during that time. When they did reach the dock, they walked off the ship onto the boardwalk, breathing in the smell of sand and palm trees. The white sand was a stark contrast to the aqua ocean. Palm trees were everywhere that the eye could see. Three huts were spread out along the beach, giving privacy to their owners. One of the crew members began unloading their luggage and taking it over to the huts.

"Why only three?" Hannah asked.

"We figured you and Dom could share one," Mr. Martin said. "There are two beds. Outside it looks primitive, but inside it's fairly modern. There are even dressers and a bathroom. Afraid the toilets are rather primitive, but they work just fine."

"Share one?" she asked, cutting her eyes to Dominick, who was grimacing but remaining quiet. "What about privacy?"

"There's a privacy wall," Mrs. Martin said. "You know, one of those things you can open or collapse like they use at stores."

Hannah made a face and stomped off, sand flying as she marched across it in her flip-flops.

"She took it better than I was expecting," Mr. Martin mused.

Dominick blew out a sigh then grabbed his suitcase and duffle bag before walking into the hut. Hannah was in there already, lying on the bed and pouting angrily.

"Your luggage is outside," he said.

"Then get it for me."

He cocked an eyebrow. "Get it yourself."

"You're a guy! You're not supposed to let a defenseless woman carry her suitcases."

"I think you're far from defenseless. You're capable of carrying it five feet."

She scoffed at him then stamped past him. She yanked the door open and snatched her suitcases up from where they lay in the sand. She threw them onto her bed, sat back down and began to pout again.

"Hannah, stop being such a brat and let's just try to get along for the next week," Dominick said. "I'm willing to try if you are."

She glared at him. "I'm leaving." She grabbed her sunglasses and stormed off.

He shook his head. If he didn't kill her before the end of the first day, it would be a miracle.

Hannah walked into the hut, her skin pink from the sun. The sun had fallen hours ago, but she'd been enjoying the warmth and the feel of the sand in her toes too much to go indoors. Pulling her sunglasses off the top of her head, she glanced around and saw that there was no sign of Dominick inside the hut. Good, she thought to herself.

She tossed her glasses down and noticed he had been rummaging around in his luggage. A few magazines were poking out of the open duffle bag. Nosy, she took a step closer and peered into the bag, pulling one of the magazines out. Her brow furrowed. It was a bondage magazine with a photo of a half-naked girl with her arms raised above her head, her legs shackled, and a ball-gag in her mouth. She pulled out a few of the others and saw they were all similar. One had a picture of a girl bent over, her hair being pulled by a man standing over her as he brought a paddle down onto her nearly bare ass.

Hannah bit her lower lip. She flipped through the magazine. Some of the images made her stomach twinge, causing a stirring between her legs. The girls had their mouths open in what was either pain or ecstasy...or perhaps both. The men dominating them were attractive and had hard looks on their faces that made her wonder what it would be like to be the girl in the photo. She peered into his bag, wondering what else was in there.

"What are you doing?" a deep voice startled her. She dropped the magazines and whipped around, nearly colliding with Dominick.

"Um...nothing," she stammered.

"Really." His eyes cut to the magazines and then back to her. "A little light reading?"

"I was just curious."

"You were snooping," he corrected. "There's a difference." He tossed his towel down onto the bed and crossed his arms. "Care to explain yourself?"

"They were there?"

He nodded. "Wow," was all he said.

"You shouldn't leave your stuff lying around where anyone can see it," Hannah said huffily, crossing her arms and jutting her chin out petulantly.

Dominick narrowed his eyes. "Hannah...I have dealt with your crap since I was twelve. I have watched your father put up with your attitude, cater to you, and spoil you rotten. Now that you're twenty, not a damn thing has changed."

"What's that supposed to mean?"

"You still think you're entitled to whatever you want. You're a spoiled little brat who throws tantrums when she doesn't get her way."

"Your point being?"

Dominick picked up the magazine she was looking at with the girl being paddled on the cover. "Have you thought that maybe I own these magazines for a reason? That maybe I have more than just a passing interest and that I've actually dabbled in it myself?"

Hannah shifted her weight from one foot to the other. "So what, you're into spanking girls with paddles?"

"I'm into discipline," he said, tossing the magazine down. "It's a part of BDSM. At the moment, I'm personally strongly considering tying you down and spanking your ass."

 cs80

Hannah blinked, sure she heard him

wrong. "Excuse me?"

"You heard me."

"You can't spank me!"

"Why not?"

"Because it's rude!"

Dominick grabbed Hannah by the back of the head, holding onto her hair. She gasped softly, her heart rate ratcheting up a notch. He looked deep into her blue eyes and said sternly, "Put your hands behind your back."

A rush of arousal went through Hannah at his tone. She slowly placed her hands behind her back, gripping her elbows on either side. She watched him lean over his suitcase, rummaging around until he pulled out a tie. He turned her away from him and looped the tie around her wrists and arms, binding them in the position she had placed them in.

Dominick turned her to face him, his milk chocolate brown eyes darker, pooling with the same hard expression she'd seen on that man in the photograph, the one she'd been lusting over. She felt a tingle between her legs and moisture seeping between them. She suddenly felt very vulnerable in her bikini.

"Find anything interesting in the magazines?" he asked. "You were looking into my bag for more."

She swallowed. "I guess...maybe."

Dominick pulled his luggage off the bed

and placed a couple pillows in the middle. "Lie down."

Hannah carefully got onto the bed on her knees and lay over the pillows.

"What does 'I guess maybe' mean?"

"It was intriguing." She sucked in air as his hand connected with her bikini-clad butt. The thin micro-fiber material offered little protection, and she could feel the sting of his entire handprint on her cheek.

"Is this intriguing?"

Hannah swallowed hard. She gasped when his hand spanked her again. The tingle she'd felt between her legs was turning into a simmer. There was a feeling of helplessness that was coursing through her veins, making her skin hum and her heart thrum in her chest.

Dominick squeezed her behind. She had a perfect ass. It was tight and toned, thanks to the years of gymnastics and ballet classes that her parents had placed her in. As he ran his hand across it, she clenched and unclenched her muscles. A tiny sigh shivered from her lips. The sound of his hand smacking down across her nearly bare rear several times echoed in the tiny hut, as did her squeals. Her body squirmed around on the bed, held down by his left palm against her back. Her tiny bare feet kicked at the mattress. When he stopped, she was gasping for breath. He could see her flesh growing pink from around the edges of her bright green bikini bottoms.

"I think that you are an absolute little brat," Dominick stated. "I'd say this spanking is long overdue."

Hannah's breaths came out as shudders. The stinging across her butt was causing a fire inside her, soaking her bottoms, and making her squeeze her legs together to get some relief. Each stroke of his hand made her want to beg him to stop but plead with him to continue.

Dominick began to untie the knots holding the front and back of her bottoms together. He pulled the tiny piece of fabric away, tossing it to the floor. She had no tan lines. He ran his hand across her ass, squeezing. Hannah inhaled sharply.

"Stick your ass up," he told her. She lifted her rear, sitting up on her knees slightly. "Good girl." The sound of skin against skin reverberated off the walls as he spanked her slowly and steadily, making her gasp and grunt out loud with each crack of the palm of his hand against her ass. He turned her tan rear a bright shade of red, spanking until Hannah was whimpering and her legs were shaking from holding herself up. Little exclamations of ouch escaped her mouth occasionally, but there were no cries of pain and no pleas for him to stop. He knew he could push her, but he didn't really want to. His dick was rock hard and all he wanted to do was fuck her senseless.

Dominick massaged her warm skin, squeezing her ass cheeks and making her sigh. His hand slipped further underneath, brushing against the dripping essences coming from her pussy. "Liked that a little, did we?" he asked, teasing her opening with his finger.

Hannah gasped. "Yes."

He slid his hand down, his fingers finding her clit. A strangled moan gurgled from her throat. "Yes what?"

"Yes sir...oh my God..." She buried her face in the bed, moaning as he massaged the throbbing bud, making her body shudder. "Ooohh...oh!" She called out as the first beautiful wave crashed over her.

Dominick yanked his shorts down and got on his knees behind her. Gripping her hips, he pulled her back into him, burying himself deep inside her. Hannah cried out in pleasure. He grasped the back of her head, tugging on her hair, thrusting into her hard, his other hand gripping her bound arms. His hips slammed against her ass as he roughly fucked her, making her body shake and loud shrieks of delight echo throughout the hut.

"Are you a bad girl?" he asked, grunting softly with each thrust. "Huh?"

"Oh God...yes, sir..." She bit her lip,

breathing heavily.

He rolled her over onto her back. His mouth crushed down onto hers, his stubble burning her tiny flesh, his fingers tangling in her hair, his dick plunging deep inside her. She moaned into his mouth. Her legs wrapped around his waist as she matched his motion, thrusting her hips up to meet his, wanting every inch of him inside her.

"Look at me," he breathed huskily, biting her neck and her shoulder, leaving red marks.

Hannah opened her eyes, locking her blue ones onto his brown ones. He ripped her bikini top off. He rolled a nipple in his teeth, making her body rise up off the bed, a scream ripping out of her throat as her pussy tightened around his dick. He growled, kissing her hard, thrusting harder, and groaning deeply as he emptied his warm seed inside her. His mouth and teeth gnashed at her lips long after he was dry.

Slowly, he pulled out and began to clean off. Hannah just lay there, trying to remember how to breathe. Dominick rolled her over and untied her arms. There were pink marks crisscrossed along her skin from the tie. She slowly sat up, her heart pounding, her legs still shaking.

"Wow," she said.

Dominick gripped her by the back of the

hair, his breath hot on her skin, his stubble scratching as he leaned in. "Are you ever going to be a brat again?"

"Is every day of the week the wrong answer?" Hannah asked with a twinkle in her eye.

5 LEATHER AND SPICE

Teagan raised her eyebrows. "What do you mean, boring?"

"That came out wrong," Colton said quickly.

Teagan was sitting on the bed with her arms crossed, her blue eyes assessing her boyfriend of three years. "Then how should it have come out?"

"What I meant to say was...we aren't quite as...exciting as we used to be."

"That doesn't sound a whole lot better, Cole."

"It's just, when we first started dating everything was all wild and hot and heavy. Now not so much."

"Well, we're seniors in college now. We have a lot of stuff going on. Sex has just taken a backseat."

"I don't know," he said. "I shouldn't have said anything."

"Well, how exactly would you like me to spice things up?"

"I don't know. Dress up like a dominatrix and tie me up?" he joked.

"Only if I get to beat your ass," she retorted.

He scooted closer and put his arm around her shoulder. "Look, baby, I'm sorry. I'm a jerk."

"Yeah, you are. But I forgive you." She kissed him. He pulled her close, deepening the kiss and she pulled back. "I don't forgive you that much."

He made a face, but stood. "I gotta get to class, anyway. I'll see you later?"

"Yep."

Teagan watched him walk off. So Colton wanted to spice up their sex life. Dress up like a dominatrix and tie me up? She pursed her lips, considering that. That would definitely spice things up. She sat down at her computer and started doing some research. She was surprised by how much information there was on being a dominatrix or dominating your man. Some of the stuff was crazy and she'd never dream of even trying it. But some of it...

Teagan wandered around the adult

shop, checking out the prices on outfits.

"Looking for something specific?" the clerk asked. She held up some red lingerie. "I bought this one and my boyfriend flipped for it."

"I was looking for something a bit more...domineering."

"Ahh. New?"

"Yeah," she said. "My boyfriend of three years told me that our sex life has gotten stale. He joked that I should dress up like a dominatrix. So I did some research and now I'm really intrigued."

"It's fun," she said. "We only do it as role play, but it's a lot of fun. It's very liberating."

"What sort of things do you do?"

"Usually I tie him up and use one of these..." She walked over to another section, Teagan close behind, and held up a flogger. "On his ass and back. It doesn't take much, just a simple flip of the wrist. Um...I will usually make him go down on me. He's got a thing for feet so we do that whole thing, but not all guys do. I've used his belt on him a couple of times and I used a hairbrush and a wooden spoon before. He's a little bit of a pain fiend so he likes it a lot. I'd make sure your boyfriend likes pain before inflicting too much on him. We started to experiment with nipple clamps. He kind of likes it, but I'd probably save it for a second time with your boyfriend if you're looking to surprise him. I'd stick with tying him up and spanking him with a lightweight flogger like this one and maybe his belt if he seems to enjoy the pain. Mostly just dominate him. Let your inner bitch reign and make him do things. Don't let him dictate anything and if he tries, punish him."

"This is going to be fun," Teagan said with a grin.

"High five to that, sister."

That night, Teagan tried on the outfit she had purchased. She'd bought a leather corset that hiked her cleavage up so high her boobs nearly spilled out, a leather skirt that conformed perfectly to her backside, and knee-high boots. She looked smoking in it, her long platinum blonde hair a stark contrast against the black corset. She smiled to herself. Colton wasn't going to know what hit him.

Pun intended.

The next day, Colton received a text message from Teagan while he was in class. He checked it and it said, 'Come to my apartment after class – no questions asked.' He furrowed his brow, a little floored by the command, but simply replied with 'OK.' There was a tiny tingling in his stomach at the tone he imagined while reading her text. He could almost see her standing there with her arms crossed, one finger wagging in the air, as she firmly told him to come over and not to argue about it. He felt a shift in his groin and he snapped his attention back to physics, hoping that would make his boner go down. If anything could, that was certainly it!

After class, he gathered up all his stuff and headed over to his girlfriend's apartment. She had been renting a tiny one-bedroom apartment since the beginning of their senior year and they had idly talked about moving in together. He was pretty sure he'd blown that chance with his comment yesterday.

When he walked into the apartment, the first thing he noticed was that it was pretty dark. There were no lights on except for a few dim lamps. He tossed his bag down and walked inside. "Teagan?" he asked. "I'm here."

Teagan stepped out of the bedroom wearing high heeled black boots that went up to her knees, a mini skirt, and a corset that clung to her body like glue, showing off every beautiful curve she had. Her cleavage was fuller than he'd ever seen it before. In her hands, she held what looked like a riding crop. Colton's stomach tumbled to his feet and his groin shift from earlier came back in full force. His mouth dropped open.

"Wow," he said.

She sauntered toward him. "You've been a bad boy, haven't you Colton?"

His dick leapt at her tone and his heart stumbled in his chest. "Um..."

"Yes ma'am or no ma'am."

"Yes, ma'am...?"

"You said our sex life was stale. One is to assume it's been going stale for a while. Maybe you should have mentioned something before it got to that point. Don't you think?"

"Um...yes, ma'am."

"Take off your shoes. Actually, take everything off."

Colton kicked out of his shoes. He pulled his t-shirt over his head and then removed his jeans, setting them both onto the couch. He pushed his boxers down and pulled off his socks. He stood there in front of his girlfriend completely naked, his erection in partial bloom, and he was surprised at how vulnerable he felt.

"Place your hands behind your back."

He did as he was told.

"Come toward me."

He stepped the few feet to stand directly in front of her. She ran the crop up the inside of his thighs, across his balls, and along his dick, which bounced a little with the feeling. She locked her eyes onto his.

"You've been very naughty and deserve to be punished. Go into the bedroom and lie face down on the bed."

"Yes, ma'am." He walked off toward the bedroom, his heart hammering in his chest. His eyes fell upon the rope tied to the headboard and the flogger setting on the bed. Swallowing hard, he lied down, adjusting himself to be comfortable.

Teagan couldn't believe how hard Colton was. She couldn't believe how wet she was! She walked into the bedroom, pleased to see he had obeyed her. His skin was so white. The curse of being a physics major – nerds don't see sunlight much.

"Did you notice the rope?" she asked.

"Yes, ma'am."

"Good." She walked over and sat the crop across his back. She pulled his wrists above his head and tied the rope around his wrists. She ran her fingernails down his back, leaving a trail of red marks in her wake. Goosebumps rose across his flesh and he shivered. She squeezed his tiny little bubble butt. When she slapped it, she relished in the way it turned slightly pink and at the sharp intake of air that Colton took. Several slaps made his lily-white backside turn a nice shade of light red. The tiny grunts coming from Colton's mouth sounded greatly like sounds of pleasure.

"We should have a safe word," she

remarked, running her nails across his rear, making him gasp. "If you need me to stop at any time, just say blue. Understand?"

"Yes, ma'am."

She picked up the flogger and tested it in the air. She'd tried it out on a pillow but she was pretty sure Colton felt more than a pillow. There'd be no way to know until she tried. She swung lightly, bringing the tiny strands down with a quiet snap against her boyfriend's upturned rear.

Colton gasped softly at the feeling. It was like a ton of little stinging pricks across his butt that sunk down deep, making his dick strain against the mattress. He groaned softly as she spanked him with the instrument. The pressure building in his cock was more painful than the feeling of the spanking. He wanted relief. He couldn't even touch himself! He gasped as she flogged up his back, causing a shiver to run down his spine.

Teagan stopped and observed Colton. "How does that feel?"

"Amazing, ma'am."

"Up on your knees more."

He gratefully did so. Teagan noticed his rock hard erection between his legs, a drop of pre-cum oozing over the tip. She snapped the flogger against his butt harder this time, making him grunt and gasp. His legs quivered and she noticed he tugged at the binds on his wrist a lot more.

"Sting a little?" she asked, running her hand across his backside.

"Yes, ma'am...quite a bit."

"Good." She patted his rump. "Roll over onto your back."

Colton rolled over onto his back, the rope easily flipping to accommodate the change. He was hopeful he was going to get some relief. He watched as his girlfriend slipped her skirt up, revealing no panties underneath. She got up on her knees on the bed and swung her leg over his head. She settled herself inches from his face. He breathed in the scent of her arousal and his dick leapt.

"Please me," she told him.

He flicked a tongue forward, across her clit. Teagan gasped, gripping the headboard with both hands, a shot of liquid fire rushing through her veins. He worked relentlessly, back and forth, up and down, in small and large circles, slow and fast...it wasn't long before she was moaning and screaming, gasping and shaking as the orgasm ripped through her.

Teagan unmounted and patted his chest. "Good boy," she said.

"Ma'am?" he said. "Please. I'm so swollen..."

Teagan's eyes fell to his thick member, bright red and gasping for attention. She playfully massaged his tight balls. He moaned deeply, his body squirming under her touch. She reached up and unfastened his binds.

"Sit up," she commanded. He did as he was told. She stepped forward and turned, saying. "Unzip my corset – with your teeth."

It took some effort, but Colton managed to take the zipper in his teeth and pull it all the way down to the bottom. Teagan slipped out of it and turned to face him. Her fingers went to his light brown hair, holding it tight, and her breasts went into his face. He needed no more invitation than this, opening his mouth and taking one swollen nipple inside, his tongue and teeth stroking softly, making her sigh and shudder with first one breast and then the other.

Teagan pulled him back and sat her boot up onto the bed. "Take off my boot."

"Fingers or teeth, ma'am?"

"Fingers will be fine, Colton."

Colton slowly untied the knot and loosened the strings before pulling first one boot, and then the second, off. He watched as Teagan shimmied out of her skirt.

"Lie down on your back," she told him.

He did as he was told.

"Grip the headboard and do not let go."
He obeyed. He watched her mount him.
She slowly lowered herself down onto his
hard, awaiting dick. He groaned as his full
length slid inside her. Teagan parted her
lips, relishing in the feeling of him inside
her. She rocked her hips, thrusting,
squeezing his hips with her knees to allow
her to move harder.

"Oh God..." He gasped, gripping the
headboard tightly, groaning. She lifted
herself up and down, bouncing on his
dick, making him whimper and squirm
underneath her. His hands reached for
her and she pinned them to the mattress,
her eyes locking onto his, her body
freezing.

"What did I tell you?" she asked in a
tone that made his stomach drop.

"Grip the headboard and don't let go?"

"Yes." She got off him and rolled him
over. She picked up the crop from earlier
and snapped it across his backside. He
gasped. The second stinging strike landed
just below the first. He bit his lip,
groaning.

"Going to listen to me next time?" she
asked, cracking the crop across his
backside hard so many times they both
lost count and Colton was groaning and
squirming underneath the blows.

"Yes, ma'am!"

"Good boy." She ran her hand across

his warm, red backside. The dips and grooves where the crop made welts felt interesting on her hand and she squeezed. He sighed. It had hurt but it had also felt amazing. She rolled him back over and he winced as his backside touched the bed. "Hurt a little bit?" she asked, her hand wrapping around his half-mast dick.

"Oh god...yes...yes, ma'am...oh please don't stop..."

She stopped. "Where are your hands?"

He placed them back where they were supposed to be – gripping the headboard tightly.

"Good boy." She stroked his dick, making him sigh. She lay on top of him, kissing him deeply. Her tongue and teeth assaulted his neck and nipples, her teeth biting and tugging on one of the sensitive buds. He groaned, his body bucking at the intense feeling. She kissed down his body, enclosed her mouth around his cock, making a few strokes with his mouth before slithering back up his body and slipping him inside her.

Colton shuddered, his hands gripping the headboard so hard he was sure he was going to break it. Each thrust of Teagan's hips brought them both closer to the brink. Her breasts jiggling above his head, the feeling of helplessness he got at having to obey her, and the sting he still felt in his backside made that fire simmer slowly.

Teagan gasped, having hit just the right rhythm, his dick stroking just the right parts of her pussy. She rocked harder, moaning, throwing her head back as she thrust him further up inside her. She rested her hands against his legs behind her, rocking hard and fast. Colton closed his eyes, his mouth opening, grunts and groans escaping. She dug her nails into his thigh and she screamed out in ecstasy as her walls tightened around him. Colton's groans matched her screams as he exploded inside her.

She stood up and cleaned herself off. Colton watched her, still gripping the headboard. She looked and grinned to see he was still obeying her.

"At ease, soldier," she teased, tossing him the towel. "So how was that for spicy?"

"I think I'd like to do it again as soon as I remember how to breathe!"

6 ENTERING THE VOID

Tiger leapt up, wrapping her hands around the pole, snaking one leg around it and twirling, then letting one high heel hit the ground. She sunk to the floor, her ass sliding down the pole with her hand behind her, her breasts jiggling, the cool air circling them. Men whooped and hollered from the floor, tossing money up onto the stage. She sank to the floor in a bow and the lights went dark. The place erupted. She gathered up her money in the pale neon light from the bar, grabbed her shirt, and scurried offstage to allow the next performer to get set up.

If someone would have told her five years ago that she would be a stripper, she'd have laughed at them. But for two years now, it was how she'd been making her money and putting herself through school. It wasn't a terrible job. She wasn't crazy about lap dances, but her bouncers kept her safe. As far as establishments go, she had picked a pretty good one.

"God, Tiger, you are amazing," Nanci, one of the newer girls, said. "I don't know how you do it. You own the stage."

"Thanks." She was never sure whether that was a compliment or not, but she always took it as one.

"Tiger!" Joseph, her boss, called to her. "You got a job offer."

She raised her eyebrows. "I'm sorry?"

"Some guy asked to speak to the manager. I talked to him and he wanted to know if you do private gigs." He handed her a card. "This is his number. He said to tell you that he would pay $400 for two hours tomorrow night."

Tiger's eye nearly popped out of her head. "Holy shit."

"Holy shit is right, kiddo. Take the job. You can have the night off." He walked off.

She called the guy and found out the details about the job. She had never done a private party before, and she was interested to find out what the atmosphere would be like. She told the guy that she wouldn't do lap dances unless she could be guaranteed protection against drunk groping, and he was cool with it. He told her to arrive fifteen minutes early so she could get changed into her outfit. For $400, she didn't care if she had to start off in a bunny suit.

Tiger parked her car in the alley of an old industrial building. She knocked on the back door and was let in by a young girl.

"Here are some choices," the lady said, motioning toward a rack of leather corsets and pants. "We didn't know what size you wore."

"Um, in leather, I'm not sure." She began to get undressed. "What's with leather?"

"It's a BDSM party," the girl said. "They're all into it."

"BDSM party, huh?" She tugged the leather pants up. They were snug, but she supposed that was the point. She zipped them and found a corset that fit. "How do I look?"

"Like a million bucks." She handed her a crop. "Stand over by that door and I'll tell you when they're ready for you."

Tiger did as she was told. She examined the crop. She didn't know what she was supposed to do with that, but she would improvise. She'd never been involved with BDSM before, although it had always intrigued her.

"Now!" the girl called out to her.

Tiger walked out onto a dark stage. She leaned up against the pole, holding the crop behind her back. The lights came on and the room erupted, the people cheering. Some sexy music started to play. She placed the crop in her teeth and spun around the pole. She did her signature move of leaping up onto the pole and twirling down. She turned her back to the crowd, bending over and spanking herself with the crop. Some whistles rang out from the crowd, a few bills being tossed up.

She whipped the crop out into the crowd and saw someone catch it. She slowly unlaced the corset and let it fall. She leaned back into the pole and slid to the ground. She unzipped the leather pants. The crowd started chanting her name. She slowly shimmied out of them, revealing her thong underneath. She twirled around the pole again and gave the crowd a tiny peek at the goods before the lights went black. Everyone clapped and hollered out for her. She gathered up her stuff and scurried back into the back.

"They loved you," the girl said. She handed her the money and added, "Feel free to stick around for as long as you want. Enjoy the party. Alcohol's free."

"Thanks." She changed her clothes and

pocketed her money. She thought about leaving, but she was interested. She wandered out into the party room. Nobody seemed to recognize her with jeans and a T-shirt on and her hair up in a ponytail. That was okay with her.

The party was even more interesting than she had been expecting. There was fetish equipment set up around the room with people performing sessions in front of everyone. One guy was pouring hot wax onto a blindfolded girl's chest. Another man was whipping a girl with what looked suspiciously like the crop she had earlier.

Tiger's eyes fell upon a man sitting by himself at a table, sipping a drink. She walked over and smiled at him. "Hi," she said. "Mind if I have a seat?"

He motioned toward the empty chair. She sat down and looked out onto the crowd.

"Quite a show," he said.

She turned to him and smiled. "Thank you."

He extended his hand. "I'm Andrew."

"Tiger," she said, shaking it.

"That's your real name?"

"It's been my name for a very long time, so yes."

"So that's a no then."

She slowly smiled. He was an attractive man—round hazel eyes and light brown hair that fell just above his collar. "It's not the name my parents gave me, if that's what you're asking. But I've been using it since I left home. It's not a stage name. I use it in life, as well."

He nodded. "Thank you, by the way. I appreciate you coming out."

Tiger furrowed her brow. "You're the one I talked to on the phone."

"That I am. Did my sister pay you?"

"Yes, she did."

"Good, good."

"So...this is your party?"

"Yep."

"So why aren't you participating?"

"I'm just throwing the party," he said. "I have no one to participate with tonight, so I'm observing. I'm perfectly fine with that."

"How long have you been into...this stuff?"

"I've been involved in this lifestyle for about ten years now. Have you ever?"

"No," she said, shaking her head. "I've always been curious, though."

"Really."

"Mm-hmm."

"Care to give it a go?" he asked.

"Um...I strip in public, but I'm not much of an exhibitionist."

"My apartment is upstairs," he said. "I have plenty to work with up there."

Tiger bit her lower lip. "You're inviting me up to your bedroom?"

A smile twitched at his lips. "I suppose

that depends on how you enjoy it."

"It's tempting...."

"Safe word is red and I stop everything. Your choice, kitten."

She slowly smiled and said, "You only live once, right?"

Andrew closed the door to his apartment and flipped on the lights. It was a pretty small apartment with an open floor plan to the living room and kitchen area. She could see his bedroom from the front door.

"Is there anything that you absolutely won't do or that frightens you?" he asked as they walked toward his bedroom.

"Um, not really," she said. "I think everything is about fair game."

He turned to face her. "Well, I'll take it easy on you. Strip."

Tiger's stomach dropped to her feet. She took off her shirt and jeans, setting them in a pile. She took her bra and panties off and set those down as well.

He turned her around and pulled her hands behind her back, tying them. He also placed a cloth around her eyes, blindfolding her. "Lie down on the bed on your stomach," he said.

She did as she was told. He lifted her up onto her knees and spread her legs. He observed her for a moment. Her blonde hair was pooling around her face. Her tight ass looked very inviting. He reached out and stroked a hand underneath her, across her slit. She gasped softly. He smacked a hand down across her ivory ass, leaving a pink mark. He picked up a soft, stringy whip. He gave her a fairly gentle test swat with it.

Tiger inhaled sharply at the feeling of each string swiping across her skin at the same time. The second one was harder, and the third one was finally the hardest, each string stinging and digging into her flesh. She gasped. She felt very exposed and open to him—vulnerable and helpless. Her breasts were squished against the mattress and her ass in the air. She knew her pussy was in full view and each stroke with the whip was making her a little wetter.

Andrew stroked the whip slowly across the moisture between her legs. He lightly tapped it against her pussy, each string nipping at the sensitive flesh, making her muscles in every part of her body clenched.

"Oh God...." She bit her lip.

"You seem to be enjoying yourself."

"Mm-hmmm...."

"I believe 'yes, Master' would be the proper response."

"Yes, Master."

He brought the whip down across her back and she moaned. He whipped it from the top of her back down to her ass again and across her thighs. She whimpered.

Andrew rolled her over onto her back and pushed her legs up, spreading them again. He ran a finger across her quivering pussy, making her tensed up. "You seem pretty wet," he said, sliding a finger inside her.

"Oooh...."

"How does that feel?" He slid his fingers across her clit, making a gurgled moan escape from her throat. He stroked softly and slowly, making her whole body shiver. "Hmm?"

"Amazing, Master...."

He kissed her inner thigh, biting softly, suckling the skin until it turned pink before moving onto another section of the thigh.

Tiger squirmed underneath his touch, aching for release, her essence dripping between her legs and her stomach swarming with butterflies of anticipation.

"So I have two things I'm considering doing next," Andrew said. "I'm considering either placing clamps on your nipples or inserting a large dildo into your pussy and making you hold it there while I whip you some more."

She bit her lower lip. "You can't do both?"

He slowly grinned. He liked this girl. He nabbed some clamps, a dildo, and a single stringed whip. He pulled her to the edge of the bed by her legs and to her feet. He untied her wrists and retied them in front, giving her enough slack to hold herself up. He pinched both nipples, rolling them in his fingers, until they were hard. Then, he placed a clamp over on, making her inhale sharply, and then the other. Each clamp sent a shot of liquid fire through her blood, straight down to her pussy.

"How does that feel?" he asked.

"Good, Master."

Andrew turned her around and pushed her to bend her over. She held herself up with her bound hands. He spread her legs.

"Stick your ass out," he said. She obeyed him, opening herself up to him. He picked up the thick dildo and slowly slid it inside her. She moaned as the rubbery surface rubbed against her walls. "Tighten to keep it in." She did so. "I'm going to whip you and you're to keep it inside until I tell you otherwise. Understood?"

"Yes, Master."

He began to whip her, starting with her ass, getting her used to the bite of the single string. She gasped and whimpered. The sting was intense, making her feel like a fire was lit across every lash. He went easier on her thighs and back, but when he whipped her ass, it made her groan and yelp. Her legs shook with the effort of keeping the dildo inside her. She could feel the pressure building. No matter how much the whip hurt, it made a fire grow inside her belly that slithered its way down between her legs. She didn't want the dildo inside her. She wanted him inside her.

When the whipping stopped, Tiger let out a deep breath.

"Push it out," he told her. She did so. He pulled it out the rest of the way, tossing the soaking wet instrument to the side. He ran his hand across her battered ass, feeling the warmth radiating from her skin. His dick was straining against his pants. He ran his hand underneath her, removing the clamps. She sighed a little as his fingers rubbed the tender flesh. The blood began to rush back to them, making them tingle and hurt.

"Oh God...." She sighed. "Master...please...."

"Please what?"

"Please fuck me."

He needed to hear no more than that. He unzipped his pants and pushed them down. He pulled her hips back into him, burying himself deep inside her. She let out a long moan. He dug his fingers into her hips, thrusting up inside her, grunting softly with each slap of his thighs against hers. He reached back, grasping her hair, tugging on it. She moaned and gasped loudly, holding nothing back as he fucked her. She groaned as she came, her walls shuddering around his thick cock.

Andrew pushed her down onto the bed and rolled her over onto her back. He ripped the blindfold off and looked down into her deep blue eyes as he entered her. His hands grasped her arms, holding her firmly against the bed. His tongue flicked across a still sensitive nipple.

"Oooh...oh God...." She moaned, writhing underneath him, her lips parting and her eyes closing. She rose up off the bed, trying to take as much of him in as she could. He complied, pushing a leg up by her shoulder, driving his full length into her, making her scream, her body shuddering and her breathing coming out in short gasps.

"Say my name," he growled. "I want to hear you scream it."

"Oh...! Oh, Andrew.... Oh my God!" She cried out as the waves crashed over her, sending her to a whole new height of ecstasy. Andrew groaned softly as he emptied himself inside her.

Tiger just lay there, trying to remember how to breathe, as Andrew cleaned himself off. He tossed the towel to her and then untied her. She blinked a few times, looking over at him in shock.

"Was it good for you?" he joked.

"Wow," she said.

"Got a little more than you bargained for when you agreed to this job, huh?"

"No shit," she said. "And here I thought $400 was a good deal. Remind me to take private jobs for you more often!"

7 NEW GUIDE TO ANATOMY AND PHYSIOLOGY

Jillian sat in her biology class, her eyes following her professor's every movement. Joseph Brown was tall with broad shoulders that stretched the backs of his button down shirts that conformed just right to what looked like muscular arms. His black slacks hung just right against his ass. His face was youthful for a man pushing forty.

His silver-rimmed glasses made him look distinguished and more intelligent than he already was. His brown hair was always impeccably trimmed and his eyes were a gorgeous shade of chocolate brown. His voice was deep and his tone never wavered. She loved how he never questioned himself and he kept the class in line. There was no talking in Brown's biology class. If you talked, you were called out and if you did it more than once, you were told to leave and come back when you were more mature. The first time Jillian had gotten raked over the coals for being late to his class she'd known she was madly in lust with the man.

"That's all for today," he said. "Don't forget your assignment is due on Monday and I won't accept any late assignments, so get it done. Have a good weekend."

Jillian placed her books in her bag slowly, her eyes scanning down her professor's body as he erased the whiteboard. Biting her lower lip, she exhaled deeply before hoisting her bag over her shoulder and walking out.

"Hey, about tomorrow night," her friend Hannah said, walking up to her. "Keith and I are going out, so..."

"Keith could come with us."

"He doesn't like the bar scene."

"So what, you're just ditching me for him? Thanks a lot, Han."

"It's still new. I'm just trying to make a good impression."

"Well, in making that good impression, don't forget about your friends."

"I'll make it up to you."

She and Hannah were supposed to go out on the town and get ridiculously drunk. It had been a long time since

Jillian had cut loose. Ever since she'd switched to pre-med, she'd been working non-stop.

"I know, I know. But this time is different."

"I'm still going out," she stated. "If you and Keith decide to have some fun, you can join me."

"Thanks, Jill."

"Yeah, yeah. I'm raiding your closet and stealing the sexiest thing I can find."

"I wouldn't have it any other way."

"Keith better give you some seriously good ass for this, that's all I have to say!"

Jillian walked into the bar wearing a short black shirt, a tank top that made her large breasts practically spill out, black socks that went up to her knees and strappy high heels that made her taller than she was. She sat down at the bar and ordered a drink. The bartender didn't card her. They never did here. She was only a few months away from twenty-one, anyway. One drink wouldn't do her any harm.

One drink turned into many as the night trudged on. She was starting to discover that drinking, and even getting drunk, was just not the same by herself. She wasn't comfortable enough to get up with strangers and dance, so she spent the whole night sitting at the corner of the bar, watching everyone else have fun and hoping desperately that her friend would show up.

"Whiskey on the rocks," a familiar deep voice said from beside her, the barstool creaking as the man sat down.

She slowly turned to face him. "Professor Brown?"

He glanced over at her. Slowly he looked her up and down, his eyebrows rising. "Jillian."

"Wow." She laughed shortly. He was wearing jeans and his infamous button down. He looked hotter than ever. "Fancy meeting you here."

"Same to you. Enjoying yourself?" he asked, a little dryly.

"Absolutely!"

His eyes fell upon her half-empty glass. "What are you drinking?"

"A little bit of everything."

"How many have you had exactly?"

"Uh...a lot," she said.

"Are you old enough to drink, Jillian?"

"Of course I am." She giggled a little, playing with the straw in her drink. She leaned over and whispered. "No, not really."

Joe shook his head lightly.

"I'm a really, really bad little girl. Maybe you should spank me."

He cocked an eyebrow. "I may be the wrong person to be telling that to." He took his drink when the bartender sat it down and took a sip.

"Why?"

Joe locked his eyes onto Jillian's. Her smile slowly faded as she watched his eyes darken as they searched her face. He finished his drink, his eyes never leaving hers. He leaned in, his breath hot against her skin as he whispered in her ear, "Because I'm liable to do just that."

"You wouldn't dare."

"You may not want to make that bet, sweetheart." He sat his credit card down and told the bartender, "For mine and pay off the young lady's tab." He turned to her and said, "If you really want a good spanking, you're coming home with me."

Jillian blinked a few times. Had he just invited her over? And threatened to spank her? Suddenly she felt very sober. And very wet.

She watched as Joe signed the receipt and stood up. "Come on," he said in that tone that made her knees weak. She slowly stood and followed him, having no idea what it was that she had just gotten herself into, but wanting to find out.

They got into his car and he shut the door. His eyes wandered the length of her. "Take your panties off," he said.

Her stomach leapt at the command. She

hesitated, but lifted her butt out of the seat and slipped her hands inside her skirt, pulled her black panties down and off.

"Good girl." He turned the ignition over on the car and pulled out of the parking lot.

Joe lived in a nice suburb on the outskirts of downtown. The house was small and lived- in but clean. Jillian's eyes wandered across the leather furniture as her professor took his shoes off.

"This way," he told her, walking past her. "Keep your shoes on."

She followed him into the spacious living room. He was sitting on the arm of the couch, watching her, his eyes never leaving hers as she crossed the room.

"Take off your shirt," he said. "Slowly."

Jillian's stomach twisted with desired at the command and her pussy tingled. She slowly pulled the tank top over her head and tossed it to the floor.

"Don't do that. Fold it neatly and set it on the coffee table."

She swallowed, folding her tank top and doing as he said.

"Come here," he said.

Jillian walked over and stood in front of him. She watched his eyes assess her, dragging down across her body.

"Take off your bra."

She unsnapped the bra, her breasts jiggling as the support came off. She folded the garment and placed it on top of her shirt.

"Lift up your skirt, bend over, and place both hands flat against the coffee table, spread your legs, and stick your ass up in the air."

Jillian swallowed hard and did as she was commanded. Cool air swirled around her, tightening her nipples and sending a cold chill down her spine. Joe stood over her, his eyes taking stock her, making her feel very vulnerable.

"You're a beautiful young lady," he told her.

"Thank you."

The next chill that shivered through her had nothing to do with the cold as Joe ran a finger down her spine. "So you want me to spank you, hmm?"

She bit her lower lip, saying nothing.

"Answer the question, Jillian."

"If you want to."

"Have you been bad?"

"Yes."

His hand ran across her smooth ass, making her heart thump in her chest. "Then you deserve a spanking, don't you?"

"Mm-hmm..."

"What else do you deserve, Jillian?" His

fingers brushed across her exposed, wet opening, making her jump in surprise. "Do you think you'll be a good girl after your spanking?" He slipped a finger inside her. She gasped. His hand slapped her cheek as his finger wiggled around inside her. "Hmm?"

"Mm...maybe."

"Oh, there will be no maybes in this household, young lady," he stated, spanking her again, harder. Jillian moaned as he slid two fingers inside her, twisting them around. "And you'd better show me a little more respect."

"Oh God...yes, sir..."

He spanked her again, his fingers working their way in and out of her trembling pussy, each stroke of his long digits causing shudders to quake through her body. "You're going to be a very good girl after this, aren't you, Jillian?"

"Yes, sir," she breathed out, gasping as his hand slapped down across her rear, squeezing, rubbing away the sting, before spanking her again. She could feel the fire simmering inside her, bubbling to the surface. His fingers continued to stroke her insides as his thumb found her clit. She groaned, squeezing her legs together. When his hand struck her backside this time, it made her yelp out in pain.

"Legs apart," he told her firmly. "Don't make me tell you again."

Her stomach took a small nosedive at his tone and she snapped her body back into position.

"Good girl," he said, his hand swatting down again, softer, rubbing afterward. He reached underneath her, his hands finding her tangling breasts, pinching her nipples, rolling them between his fingers and making her whimper and shudder.

"Stand up," Joe told her.

She did as she was told, turning to face him. She watched as he unbuckled his belt and pushed his jeans down. His impressive erection was already protruding from his boxers, a drop of pre-cum threatening to spill over the edge. He pulled his boxers off and sat down on the couch.

"On your knees."

Jillian knelt in front of him. He took her head and pulled her down to his dick, touching her lips against the head. She opened her mouth, letting him in. His fingers held her head tightly as his hand guided her, giving her no control as he moved her up and down. He groaned softly as her tongue massaged the sensitive flesh, his sounds of pleasure wanting her to give him more but his hold on her making it impossible. He pulled her up, his hand clutching her brown hair tightly, making her look up into his lust-filled eyes.

"On the couch," he said, pointing toward the arm. She sat down. "Scoot down further and open your legs. That a girl. Now touch yourself."

Jillian placed her fingers against her clit, rubbing slowly, sending a wave of pleasure through her body. She kept her eyes on Joe as she did it. The way he watched her made her gasp and shiver, fueling the flame licking at the surface, struggling to break through.

"Stop," he told her just short of her coming. She whimpered a little, but did as she was told.

"Take off the rest of your clothes."

Jillian slowly stripped off her shoes, socks, and skirt, making sure to place them neatly on top of her tank top. Joe stepped up behind her, running his hands across her stomach. His hand pushed her down until she was bent over. She rested her hands back against the coffee table, instinctively spreading her legs, giving him a good view of her throbbing sex. He brushed a hand across it, making her sigh. He slid his dick inside her slowly and she tightened around him, gasping as the length of him entered her fully. She squeezed her eyes shut as he stayed inside unmoving for a moment, filling her, stretching her. His hand smacked down on her rump and she cried out in a mixture of pleasure and pain, her legs squeezing shut.

"Keep them apart," he reminded. "Break position again and I'll use the belt on you."

She shuddered as he pulled out. "Yes, sir." She spread her legs again, willing herself to stay in position as he teased her opening. "Please, sir..."

"Please what?"

"Please fuck me...I just want to cum...and I want you so bad."

He spanked her again, making her bit her lip. "You're the one who wanted to be spanked."

"Mm...yes, sir. Ooh..." She squeezed her eyes shut as he slid back inside. Her fingernails scratched against the coffee table.

"Finger your clit," he told her.

Jillian gratefully slid a finger between her folds, massaging the engorged bud. Joe didn't move, his thick cock hard and throbbing inside her, as she masturbated. His fingers squeezed her nipples and his free hand spanked her ass hard. She gasped softly as the pleasure built up inside her.

"Don't cum," he warned her.

"Oh, please, sir..."

"Stop," he said.

She whined a little, but did as she was told. She ached for release. Her whole body longed for it, her skin humming and her pussy quivering in desire.

Joe pulled out of her and turned her around. He shoved her up against the wall, his hands pinning her wrists above her head. "You listen very well," he stated. "Have you done this before?"

"No, sir."

His dick brushed against her leg as he leaned in, biting her neck. "I'm very surprised." He looked deep into her eyes. "You're a natural."

"Thank you, sir."

"Do you want to cum?" he asked her, flicking a tongue across her hard nipples, making her whimper.

"Oh god, yes, sir...so badly."

"Do you want me to fuck you?"

"Yes, sir."

He hoisted her up, burying himself deep inside her, making her cry out in pleasure, gripping his shoulders. He thrust up inside, slamming her back against the wall, grunting as he drove into her. Jillian's fingernails dug into his shoulder, her cries and moans increasing as her pussy squeezed him tight, the waves crashing over her, taking her higher and higher until her screams echoed through the house.

Joe wrapped his arm around her waist, swinging around and pushing her down onto the floor, the force of his movements causing the harsh carpet to burn her skin. Her hands hit the floor, her back arching up to meet him.

"Scream my name," he growled, his teeth tugging on the flesh of her neck and the sensitive skin on her breasts.

"Oh god, Joe...oh god, yes!" she cried out, her nails digging into the carpet as she came, her legs shaking with the power of each one. His mouth crushed down on hers, his tongue possessively taking her to new heights, draining every ounce of energy out of her until her body was spent. She shuddered as she felt his warmth fill her.

Joe stood and cleaned himself off before handing her the towel. She weakly took it, breathing heavily, staring at the ceiling.

"Stand up, Jillian," he told her.

She dragged herself to her feet and cleaned herself off. She handed the towel back to him.

"You really are a natural."

"And I guess being a biology professor has paid off," she said breathlessly.

8 SHOWING HER THE ROPES

Rylee stared at her reflection in the mirror, sighing deeply. Her blonde, purple, and pink dreadlocks stared back at her, her blue eyes hidden behind sunglasses. She ripped them off and tossed them down. She was twenty-one years old and felt like her life was going nowhere.

"What's wrong with you?" Mandy, her gothic roommate, asked. Mandy wore dark purple or black clothes and had her long black hair stick straight all the time.

"My life sucks."

"Everyone's life sucks. That's the point."

"No, I mean...every guy I date is a loser. School blows big ones. My car is a piece of shit. And I can't even get a job because my stupid school schedule won't allow any free time unless I want nothing of a life. And I can't remember the last time I got laid."

"That does suck."

"Exactly."

"You need to stop moping, though. Christ, Rylee, I'm the Goth chick and I'm less depressing than you are."

"That's because you're not a real Goth chick."

"We aren't all depressed and want to cut ourselves."

"Whatever you say, Mandy."

"You know, I was thinking about going out to a club later. Would you like to come with?"

"What kind of club?"

"It's called The Cross. It's a fetish club."

"You mean like where they have people being whipped and stuff? Like...S&M shit?"

"Exactly," she said. "One of the girls in my art class goes there all the time. I hear it's pretty wild. I think we'd fit in well. We're both pretty freaky. And who knows—maybe you'll find the man of your dreams."

"I don't want the man of my dreams. I just want someone who can get me off."

That wasn't the full truth. Rylee wouldn't mind a guy who could sweep her off her feet. She just didn't believe in that kind of thing. As far as she was concerned, love didn't exist and price charming was just a fairy tale. But if she could find someone to satisfy her for once, that would be enough until some semblance of prince charming came along.

Rylee got dressed up in the sluttiest thing she could find in her closet, which ended up being a purple plaid pleated skirt that landed just south of her ass and a purple corset that hoisted her boobs up enough to make her cleavage look pretty damn impressive. Mandy wore standard black and combat boots. Rylee was pretty sure that Mandy didn't own anything but black and purple with the occasional splash of red thrown in for good measure.

They instantly got let into the club. Wearing slutty clothes sometimes had its advantages. There was industrial music booming from an overhead speaker. A few groups were dancing. Most people were talking. There were a few people Rylee could tell were just there for the atmosphere and some were just playing a part. Then there were some she could tell were hardcore players. They would speak and disappear into the backroom. Rylee wondered what kinds of things went on in the backroom. She guessed it was filled with equipment that could be used by the patrons. Her stomach quivered slightly as she imagined the things that could be going on back there.

Rylee ordered a drink. She scanned the room for an empty table. Her eyes fell upon a man sitting alone, nursing a drink, scanning the room. He had long jet-black hair and stark blue eyes she could see from a distance. His shoulders were broad and his exposed upper arms were muscular and rippled slightly every time he raised his arm to take a drink. He locked eyes with her as she approached him.

"Hi," she said with a smile. "Can I sit down?"

"Go ahead," he said, his voice laced with an Australian accent.

She sat down. "I'm Rylee, by the way."

"Everett."

"Nice to meet you, Everett. I like your accent."

"Thank you."

"So do you come here often?" she asked, taking a sip of her drink.

"Now and again," he replied. "You?"

"This is my first time here. My roommate wanted to come and wanted some company, so I came with."

"Are you involved in the lifestyle?"

"No," she said. "It's curious, though. I have to admit that I'd like to explore it a bit. My sex life is usually pretty boring and standard. I think spicing things up a bit might be interesting."

"Is that so?"

"Mm-hmm." She finished her drink and looked at him with a smile. "So are you involved in the lifestyle?"

"I've been around the block a few times. Would you like me to show you around?"

"I have been wanting to know what goes on in the back."

"I can show you," he said. "We can experiment a bit, if you'd like."

Rylee's stomach dropped to her feet. She bit her lip. "Maybe I'll take you up on that."

Everett showed Rylee around the club. They entered the backroom, which was basically a hallway that led to other rooms. "There are about ten other rooms," he said. "Each one has slightly different equipment, but anyone who knows what they're doing can do just about the same thing in each room." He stopped in front of an open door and turned to her. "Care to give it a go?"

"You know what you're doing?"

"I've been doing this for a long time, pet. Yes, I do."

She gnawed on her lower lip.

"We can take it easy," he said. He slipped an arm around her waist and added, whispering into her ear, "And if you want, I live within walking distance." He locked eyes onto hers. He leaned in, his lips brushing against hers. His tongue slipped inside, stroking against hers softly, making her sigh. He stepped around her, inside the room.

Rylee exhaled deeply and walked into the room, shutting the door behind her.

"So, um...now what?" Rylee asked, suddenly a little nervous.

Everett stepped forward, securing a collar around her neck. He snapped a leash onto it and gave it a tiny tug. She followed him around the room, over to a chair. He sat down and said, "Take off your top."

She did as she was told. His eyes dragged up and down her curves, taking in her beautiful, supple breasts. He picked up a pair of handcuffs and cuffed her hands behind her back. He leaned forward, kissing her neck, biting the flesh between her neck and shoulder. "Ever been tied up before?"

"Once," she said. "It wasn't very sexy."

"Spanked?"

"My dad used to whip my ass with a leather belt. Does that count?"

"Most definitely not." He pulled her down over his lap. "We'll take it easy on you. Maybe we'll try something else once we get back to my place." He flipped up her skirt and slipped his fingers inside the hem of her panties, pulling them down to her ankles. His hand caressed her white backside, making her sigh softly. He wrapped an arm around her waist, underneath her bound wrists, locking her against him. When Everett's hand connected with her bottom, she gasped softly. He ran across her bum, rubbing. Then he began to slowly spank her, softly at first and then gradually increasing the intensity.

Each crack of his hand felt like a strike of lightning straight to Rylee's center. Her pussy throbbed in tune with the stinging burn in her backside. She wanted to be fucked. She squirmed to get some relief without any luck. Her tiny gasps and moans egged Everett on. He knew she was enjoying it. He knew she wanted sexual relief. But he was relishing in her sounds; in the way her ass bounced as he spanked it and the beautiful red color it was turning. The torture of it was sweet. Her whimpers and whines made him hard.

Everett stopped, rubbing his hand up and down her warm rear, making her shudder. "How did that feel?"

"Oh my God...it hurt...but it felt...amazing."

He could feel her moisture soaking

through to his pant leg. Relief would come soon enough. But for now...

He stood her up and pushed her down to her knees. He tipped her head up to face him. He reached out, cupping both her breasts, skimming his thumbs across her hard nipples. She gasped a few times before biting her lip and closing her eyes, drinking in the sensation. His fingers rolled the sensitive nubs, squeezing, twisting, tugging, and torturing until Rylee was whimpering.

"I think you like being tortured," Everett mused. His teeth scraped across her nipple, biting, making her gasp. "Don't you?"

"It doesn't suck," she said breathlessly.

He unzipped his pants and pulled out his dick. She licked her lips, her eyes falling upon his hard, beautiful member. He grasped her dreadlocks and pushed her head down to it. "Lick it," he said.

The commanding tone of his voice sent a skitter through her belly. Her tongue reached out, flicking across the head, taking a healthy taste of him. Swirling around the top and then underneath, she soaked in the small grunts that rumbled from his throat as she lapped at his dripping dick.

He pulled her down further, pushing the length of him inside her mouth. She opened herself up, taking him to the base of her throat, moaning softly as she felt a surge of submission at his leading her. Her head bobbed lightly, her pussy aching for release as she felt his swelling inside him. He tightened his grip on her hair, the pulling deliciously painful. His hand thrust her up and down, making her fuck him with her mouth. Everett groaned deeply as he exploded inside her mouth. Rylee gulped down every last bit she could manage to. He released his hold on her hair and she slowly pulled away, letting his limp member fall to his leg.

"You're a very beautiful young woman," he told her, reaching out and wiping her mouth. He pulled her up to her feet and observed her quiet submission. "That invitation back to my apartment is still open. I'd very much like to tie you down to the bed and have my way with you."

Rylee bit her lip. "And I would very much love for you to do that."

Rylee tugged on the binds holding her to the headboard of Everett's queen sized bed. She was stripped naked with her wrists tied to the metal rails. Her legs were suspended above her, shackled to a suspension bar, holding her spread eagle. She watched as Everett stripped naked. His chest and abs were as beautiful as his shoulders and arms. His thighs were thick and toned. And that dick of his...it made Rylee wet just looking at it. The fact that it was rock hard again already made her mouth water.

Everett picked up a flogger and ran it up between her legs and up her belly. "You liked getting spanked, didn't you?"

"Mm-hmm...yes, sir."

He flogged her ass and she sighed in pleasure. "You like that, too?"

"Yes, sir...oh!" She gasped as he flogged her hard. Her moans and gasps echoed throughout the room as the leather strings slashed down across her ass several times.

Everett brought the flogger down lightly across one of Rylee's breasts.

"Ooh!" She gasped, opening her eyes and watching as the thin strings lashed across her other breast, leaving pink marks. He tapped the flogger against her wet sex, his eyes meeting hers. Seeing the lust behind them, he flogged her pussy, making her moan and yank at her binds, rising up off the bed.

"Does that feel good?" he asked.

"Oh god, yes...oh...!" She threw her head back, moaning as the sharp lashes against her pussy and clit pushed her over the edge, and her walls shuddered inside her.

Everett took a step back, grinning a

little. He'd never made a girl cum by whipping her before. He'd heard of it happening but he'd never found a girl that was that into it. He stroked his hand across his throbbing dick as his eyes wandered down Rylee's battered body. Her ass and breasts were covered in whip marks. Her face looked positively serene.

He tossed the flogger down and got up onto the bed, his ass end at Rylee's face. He touched his dick to her lips and she parted them, taking him in. He dipped his head down, his tongue flicking across her clit. She moaned around his dick, moving her head forward and back. The way her throat rumbled as he lapped at her pussy made him groan softly. He pulled out and stood up. He unhooked her legs and slipped between them, up to her face. His mouth crushed down on hers, kissing her deeply, passionately, possessively. Rylee whimpered into his mouth, melting as his tongue brushed against hers roughly. He kissed around her neck, biting, sucking, and nibbling his way down to her breasts. His tongue and teeth tormented the already sensitive flesh, leaving her crying out in pleasure.

"Do you want me to fuck you?" he whispered in her ear, his teeth nipping at the cartilage. "Hmm?"

"Oh god, yes."

Everett spread her legs, sliding his hard

dick inside her. She was so wet he nearly fell out. He thrust up inside, hard, pushing himself all the way inside her, taking her to the base. Skin slapped against skin as he drove into her, his hips rocketing against hers, making her yell out his name. She pulled at the shackles, the scream ripping from her throat as she squeezed him tight.

"Yeah," he said, growling softly, kissing her neck. "That's it. That's a good girl." He kissed her, wrapped his arms around her legs, pushing them up around his shoulders as he thrust into her.

"Oh my god...oh...!" Rylee's legs shook and her body trembled. Every nerve ending felt as if it had burst to life at once. Every stroke of his dick, every touch of his fingers, and every lap of his tongue made her moan in delight. Her body ached from every wave of pleasure and every hard thrust up inside her. She wanted it to end, but yet she wanted it to last forever.

"Cum for me," Everett said, his accent sending shivers down her spine. "Cum for me, pet."

"Mmmm..." Rylee whined, her throat hoarse from screaming, and she merely moaned softly instead as her pussy gripped her lover's dick tightly. Everett groaned, exploding inside her. He kissed her deeply, staying inside her as he went limp, his tongue stroking hers until she was whimpering.

Everett's eyes scanned Rylee's body, admiring his handiwork. Her head lulled back and forth, her eyes fluttering open. He grinned a little. "How was that for your first experiment with the lifestyle?"

"Mm...I think as soon as I'm able to move and breathe again, we should continue the experiment." She grinned wickedly.

"I think you may be right."

9 BOUND DESIRE

Piper tossed her book bag down on the floor beside her bed and flopped down onto her back on the mattress. She stared up at the ceiling. Finals were almost over. She couldn't wait for summer! It was the end of her first year of college, and she hadn't been sure if she would survive. It had been brutal and she was questioning why she'd ever decided to become a radiology technician.

The only upside to the whole thing was that her boyfriend, Sawyer, went to the same university at the graduate school across campus. When she'd been accepted into the university, she had been ecstatic. She and Sawyer had only been going out for five months when she'd applied, and she couldn't believe her luck. Her parents loved him because he was sweet and gentle. She also loved him, but there were things about Sawyer that she didn't love, one of those things being the fact that he was sweet and gentle.

There was a short rap on the door. Piper leapt to her feet and rushed over, throwing it open. A grin broke across her face when she saw Sawyer standing on the other side. He stepped inside and shut the door behind him, gathering her up into his arms and kissing her.

"How long 'til your roommate gets back?" he asked.

"Not for at least an hour or two."

"Should be enough time." He grinned, biting her lower lip teasingly.

She giggled, wrapping her arms around his neck, kissing him. He picked her up and carried her over to the bed, lying on top of her. She nuzzled against his neck, breathing in the musky smell of his cologne. Sawyer's hands skimmed down the length of her dress, tickling her rib cage on the way down. She squirmed under his touch, letting out a tiny murmur. He slid his hands underneath the soft fabric, pushing it up her thighs, under her rump. His lips skimmed across her stomach as the dress went up further. Soon the pink garment was in a heap on the floor, leaving her lying there in her matching colored satin panties and bra.

"Cute," he said, placing a hand over her breasts, brushing a thumb across the top of the mound until the nipple stiffened underneath. A shudder ran through Piper's body, raising gooseflesh all along her body. Sawyer leaned down, kissing her chest, running his hands behind her back to unsnap her bra. He tossed the bra beside her dress. His hands squeezed her breasts, his eye locked on hers as he kissed up the middle of her chest to her mouth. Piper sighed, closing her eyes, drinking in the feeling.

Sawyer's tongue caressed hers as his fingers tweaked her nipples, causing small jolts of pleasure to rush through her veins. She brought her knee up, brushing it against the bulge in his slacks. A deep groan rumbled out of his throat and he pulled her closer. Deepening the kiss, his hand rushed down her back to yank the satin panties away from her, down her milky white legs. He shed his clothes and was instantly on top of her, probing her entrance teasingly, a playful grin on his face.

As he entered her, Piper bit her lower lip and dug her nails into his shoulders. Her lips parted as a moan shuddered out. Each languish movement, each slow rock of his hips, brought her closer and closer to the brink until the feeling broke over her like a tidal wave and she cried out. His kisses drowned out her moans until he groaned with his own burst of release.

Piper rolled over in bed and watched Sawyer as he rummaged in her laundry basket for a towel. He had a cute butt. It was the first thing that had attracted her to him. Then she had seen his face – that nicely chiseled jaw reminded her of a movie star's. He had black hair that was wavy and always tussled by the wind and it fell into his gorgeous green eyes.

The sex was never a real issue with Sawyer. It was good, she nearly always made it to the big O, and it was never a contest to see who could outdo the other. But, Piper had fantasies. She had always had them and she'd always been afraid to bring them up to her boyfriends; Sawyer was no exception.

Sawyer pulled on his slacks and leaned over, kissing her, letting it linger a few moments. He pulled back and smiled at her. "You look really nice today," he told her.

"Don't I every day?" she teased.

"But of course!" He pulled his shirt on and took her hands, pulling her to her feet. "I was thinking maybe we could go to dinner tonight. Finals are over for me and you've only got one more left, right?"

"Right."

"It's your blow off class, isn't it?"

"Yep!"

He wrapped his arms around her waist, drawing her close. "So is it a date?"

Piper stood on her tippy toes and kissed the tip of his nose with a grin. "Absolutely."

Sawyer kissed her lips before heading for the door. "I'll come by around 8. Is that okay?"

"Sounds great!"

She watched him leave and blew out a sigh. Maybe by tonight, she'd be able to summon the courage to finally bring up what she wanted. She could see Sawyer being the one. Past boyfriends who were nothing more than a fleeting thing – not sharing her secret with them wasn't a problem for her. But how could she go into a long-term relationship with someone she truly cared for, could feel herself falling deeply in love with, without telling him exactly what she yearned for?

Piper was applying the last of her mascara when there was a rap on the door.

"I'll get it," Kami, Piper's roommate, called from the living area of the tiny studio apartment that they shared.

"Thanks." She took a step back and examined herself in the full-length mirror. The little black dress molded perfectly to every curve of her body. Her usually straight brown hair fell in soft ringlets around her shoulders. The deep purple eye shadow she'd chosen was striking against her deep brown eyes. She smoothed her hands down her sides, turning and examining herself one last time before stepping out into the living area.

Sawyer was wearing jeans and a black sport jacket over a blue button-down. His unruly hair was brushed back and gelled to maintain control. He looked sexy as ever. His eyes wandered down the length of her and then slowly back up, his mouth parting a bit, before a small smile played at his lips. "You look amazing," he said.

She grinned. "Thanks. You don't look too shabby yourself." She turned to Kami and said, "Don't wait up."

Sawyer drove them to a tiny bistro on the other side of town. It was a quaint little place they had been to before. It was nice and quiet and allowed for conversation amid gentle live acoustic music in the background.

"You look really nice," Sawyer remarked, his eyes skimming down her face to her breasts and back up. "It's a cute dress. Is it new?"

"It's Kami's," she said. "But it fits pretty well."

"I'll say."

"You just like how it accents my boobs."

"I am a guy. Of course I do."

"So you've got the place to yourself tonight, right?"

"That I do," he said with a smile.

Piper returned the smile. They would have the whole house to themselves with his parents away on business. All she would have to do is bring it up. Did she have the guts to do that?

They made small talk as they finished their dinner and dessert. Piper's stomach twisted with nervous anticipation as they neared his home. She still hadn't brought up her fantasy.

"We should have stopped and got some wine," Sawyer mused as they walked into the house.

Piper perked up. Wine would help shed her inhibitions. And it would give her some more time to figure out how to bring it up. "Isn't there a little liquor store down the road?"

"Do you want some wine?"

"I'd love some wine."

"I'll go grab a bottle. Do you want to come?"

"Nah, I'll stay here."

He gave her a quick kiss on the lips before leaving. She wandered around the living room, rolling ideas around in her head.

Ever since Piper was a teenager, she'd

had the same fantasy. She wanted a man to blindfold her, tie her up, and have his way with her. She'd never had the guts to ask any boyfriend to do it to her. But with Sawyer, it was different. She wanted him to know her every fantasy. But she was terrified of how he would react. He was so nice and sweet! Would he think she was a freak?

Piper opened her purse and pulled out the furry pink handcuffs she had purchased months ago but never brought up. She had brought them along, thinking she would get the balls to bring up what she wanted. She idly wondered what Sawyer would do if she just handcuffed herself on the bed. She bit her lip, staring down at the handcuffs. It was now or never.

She stripped down to her black bra and panties. She found a black scarf she had left in his drawer and wrapped it around her head, covering her eyes. She fumbled with the handcuffs a bit but managed to get them locked around her wrists behind her back. She lay down on the bed on her belly and waited. The adrenaline was pumping through her veins. There was no backing out now.

The door clicked as Sawyer unlocked it.

A twinge of fear punched at Piper's stomach while at the same time a tingle of pleasure flushed her skin with warmth.

"Piper?" he called out, shutting the door behind him. He frowned, craning his neck around the corner of the foyer into the living room. He kicked off his shoes and made his way toward the bedroom. "Hey, hon, I got the wine." He sat it on the coffee table as he walked past. "Babe...." He stopped in the doorway.

The fuzzy pink handcuffs were a stark contrast against the black lingerie. Her milky white skin looked delicate and innocent, her beautiful brown locks flowing against her back.

"Piper?" he asked quizzically, stepping closer to the bed.

"Hi."

"Hi." He brushed some hair away from her face and noticed how red it was. "Pretty interesting look you've got going on here."

"I've been trying to figure out how to bring it up...so I thought I'd surprise you. Surprise!" she said weakly.

Sawyer nodded, frowning thoughtfully, looking at her up and down. Her plump rear looked delectable in that position. He touched her arm, running a finger along it from her shoulder to her elbow. Goosebumps instantly rose down her body.

"You don't think I'm a freak, do you?" she asked.

"Absolutely not. I think you look adorable. And pretty damn hot, for that matter." He rested his hand on her backside, squeezing lightly. Piper sighed softly. "I'm guessing there's something you have to say to me?"

She squirmed a little. "I kind of have...fantasies. Unfulfilled fantasies, shall we say."

"I'm assuming they have something to do with a blindfold and handcuffs?"

"I've always wanted to just be controlled. Not like crazy whips and chains and stuff like that, but...yeah. Blindfolded and handcuffed."

"You want to feel loss of control," he said simply.

"That's a good way to put it."

Sawyer pulled his shirt over his head. "Anything else I should know?"

"No, that about covers it."

He shed his pants. "Okay then." He hooked a hand around the handcuffs and pulled her toward the edge of the bed and up onto her feet. He removed her bra and studied her for a moment. She stood there, gnawing on her lower lip. Her face was still flushed red. Her nipples were taut and inviting. Sawyer leaned forward, flicking one with the tip of his tongue. Piper gasped out loud, not having expected it. He moved over to the other one, this time enveloping the sensitive nub into his mouth, sucking, nibbling, and licking it until she was breathing heavily and shuddering.

Sawyer sat down on the bed and hooked a finger around the hem of her panties, pulling her closer. He ran his hands up her legs, caressing her backside. He kissed her belly and down around her thigh, nibbling on the tender flesh there. His finger brushed aside her panties, probing inside, feeling how wet and warm she was for him.

"Oh..." Piper said, parting her lips, making soundless gasps.

Sawyer pulled down her panties slowly, taking his time, making her quiver with suspense. He stood, wrapping his arms around her, kissing her hard, a primal roughness behind his lips that he'd never used before. Piper melted against him, moisture seeping out between her thighs, as his fingers tangled tightly in her hair, holding her in place. He reached underneath her, fondling her, making her moan into his mouth.

"Does that feel good?" he asked huskily into her ear as he stroked against her clit.

"Oh my God, yes," she said breathlessly.

He nibbled on her neck, continuing his ministrations until he brought her right to the brink and stopped. She whined in protest. He pushed her over the bed and bent down, her face buried into the sheets with her ass up in the air. Dropping his boxers, he gripped her hips and dragged her back into him, filling her. Piper cried out in pleasure. He grunted softly as he thrust into her, the sound of skin slapping against skin echoing in the empty house. He tugged on her hair, holding onto it tightly, his other hand swatting down onto her lily-white cheek, leaving a light pink mark.

As Piper's body shuddered with a wave of pleasure, her face being buried in the sheet muffled her screams. Sawyer yanked her up to her feet and unhooked the handcuffs. He pushed her down onto her back and held a hand around her wrists. He pulled her blindfold down with his free hand, looking into her eyes. The lust filling them made his stomach twist with desire.

"Is this what you've been wanting?" he asked, teasing her with his dick, making her shiver.

"Yes."

He slid his full length slowly inside her and she gasped, closing her eyes. He pulled the blindfold back over her eyes and placed both her arms on either side of her head with his hands locked tightly around both wrists. Each hard, sharp movement brought a strangled moan from her throat. He hadn't minded being soft and sweet with her, but knowing that she wanted it rough brought things to a whole new level. He held nothing back, riding through each break and swell of passion, bringing out screams and cries of ecstasy from her he'd never heard before. Her body rose up to meet him, a light sheen of sweat covering her body. Her legs shook, hooked behind his back. She writhed underneath him, her body trembling.

"Say my name," he growled. "Scream it."

"Oh, God!" She gasped out. "Oh, Sawyer...oh my God...oh!"

Sawyer kissed her hard, groaning deeply as he emptied his seed inside her, her walls closing tightly around him, her legs squeezing around his waist, taking in every inch of him to extend the feeling for as long as possible.

They lay there for a few minutes afterward, gathering their bearings. Piper slowly reached up and pulled the blindfold off, her heart still pounding in her chest.

"If you ever have another fantasy, you need to tell me about it," Sawyer said. "Don't ever be afraid to tell me something."

She grinned a little. "Trust me...I never will again!"

10 LEARNING HOW TO BEG

"I'd like you to help out with the Miriam Foster fundraiser this weekend," Madelyn Kensington told Sienna Albright. "I think that you are one of our brightest, most promising interns. Mr. Kensington knew what he was doing when he hired you!"

Sienna grinned. "Thank you very much, ma'am. You have no idea how much I appreciate all the opportunities you folks have given me over the past two months."

"The pleasure has been ours, Sienna. Parker will be coming with you to the fundraiser. You'll be more in charge than he will. He's just there to observe and learn. You'll watch after him, won't you? Make sure he doesn't get into any trouble?"

The grin turned to a tight smile. "Absolutely."

Parker was the Kensington's twenty-four-year-old son who acted more like he was fourteen. He had no discernible skills whatsoever, unless you counted being able to do a keg stand as a skill. He'd gotten the internship for the Kensington Foundation simply because he was his parents' pet. They coddled him and it disgusted Sienna to no end. She tolerated him because she needed this internship for college credit and because it looked good on her resume. But three months of putting up with him, with another month on the plate, was becoming harder and harder. The idea of being in a car with Parker for a four-hour trip to Washington, D.C., was not a pleasant thought.

"Hey!" Parker said, bounding up next to Sienna as she headed for her car. "What time did you want to pick me up tomorrow for the trip?" he asked.

She turned to face him, a droll expression on her face. "And why am I picking you up?"

"Because my car broke down."

She cocked an eyebrow.

"Okay, fine, I got too many speeding tickets and I had my license yanked. But my car wasn't working so hot before that happened, anyway."

"God, Parker, you are so pathetic."

"That's rude! So what time?"

Running a hand down her face, she sighed deeply and said, "We'll leave at 6 a.m. We should be there before ten and that will give us a couple of hours to get ready before the fundraiser starts. Dress professionally!"

"Don't I always?"

Sienna looked him up and down with a skeptical look, taking in his tattered jeans and T-shirt. "No."

He batted those baby blue eyes, his long lashes fluttering against his tan skin, and his brown hair shimmering in the sunlight. "Aw, come on, Sienna. You know you love me."

"6 a.m.," she said. "Be ready or I'll leave without you." She got into her car and slammed the door shut.

The next morning, Sienna got up at 3 a.m. She showered, fed her cats, had a bowl of oatmeal, and opened her closet doors in search of the perfect outfit. She picked a white button-up blouse and a black skirt. She pulled on a matching black blazer and examined herself in the mirror. Perfect. She slipped on some panty hose, got into her high heels, and made herself some coffee. After throwing on the minimal amount of makeup, just enough to look a little seductive while still professional, she was out the door before 5 a.m.

She arrived in front of Parker's apartment five 'til six. She shot him a text and waited. Thirty minutes later, he finally came walking out the door. She was already fuming but her jaw hit her chest when she saw he was wearing jeans.

"Really, Parker?" she asked as he got into the passenger side.

"Sorry! I overslept."

"No. What you're wearing."

He looked down at himself. "I'm wearing a button-down!"

"And jeans."

"But they're brand new."

Sienna took a deep breath and slowly let it out. Deciding it wasn't worth it, she squealed her tires on the way out of the driveway.

They hit rush hour traffic on the way into the city. Sienna drummed her fingers against the steering wheel. Parker played with the radio.

"This sucks," he stated. "There's nothing good on. And we haven't moved for ten minutes."

"That's why I wanted to get such an early start."

"I only made us half an hour late."

"A half an hour means everything during rush hour, Parker!"

He mimicked her silently, rolling his eyes. Sienna gripped the steering wheel tightly, wishing it were his neck instead.

They arrived at the fundraiser fifteen minutes before it was about to start.

"Let me do all the talking. Just stand there and look pretty," she growled at him.

"God, you're being a bitch."

"I swear to God, if you screw this up...do not screw this up. Keep your mouth shut."

Parker had no idea what to do at the fundraiser so he mostly followed Sienna around like a lost puppy dog. When he finally got bored, he wandered off and she didn't see him for the rest of the day. It was partially a relief and the other part of her was terrified of what he might be getting into. She just hoped if he was doing something stupid, he didn't mention his parents' company in the process.

The fundraiser lasted all day and night, finally coming to a close at 8 p.m. that night. It had been successful and they'd raised over $3,000 for cancer research.

"Thank you so much for all of your help," Sienna told one of the campaign promoters.

"It was our pleasure. Please tell Mr. and Mrs. Kensington thank you for the work that they're doing."

"Will do!" Parker said, walking up, munching on some chips.

Sienna elbowed him in the side and rephrased, "We'll be sure to do that. Thanks again."

She nodded and walked off.

"Where have you been?" Sienna asked Parker.

"Wandering," he said simply. "Can we go now?"

"We need to clean up."

"You mean you need to clean up."

"Parker...I did all the damn work. The least you can do is help clean up."

"Again...bitch." He walked off.

"Aarggh!" Sienna groaned.

The clock was edging toward eleven o'clock when she finished cleaning everything up. All she wanted to do was get home to her warm bed. She couldn't find Parker anywhere and he wasn't answering her texts. She walked out to her car to find him asleep in the backseat.

"Are you shitting me?" she said out loud. She yanked the door opened and slapped his foot. "Parker!"

He jumped and looked up. "What?"

"What are you doing?"

"Sleeping. I was tired."

"You didn't do anything all day! You..." She took a deep breath. "Get your ass in the front. We're going home."

"Thank God!" He got out and into the passenger seat.

Sienna shivered, wrapping her coat

closer around her. The temperature had dropped about twenty degrees since this morning and the air felt icy and smelled of frost. She got into the driver's side and turned the engine over. She flipped on the heater and pulled out onto the road.

Half an hour into the drive, it started to snow. An hour later, they were crawling along the road in a total whiteout.

"I can't see anything," Sienna said.

"We should have just stayed at a hotel."

"Shut up! I didn't know it was going to be a blizzard out, okay?"

"Whatever!"

"You know, I'm really sick of your attitude."

"I'm sick of you being such a bitch."

"Stop calling me a bitch, Parker! It's disrespectful and unprofessional."

"Well, then maybe you should stop being one."

Sienna was about to say something when her car hit a patch of ice and skidded. She jerked her wheel, trying to regain control of the car. The bumper hit the guardrail and spun out, crashing over the side of a weak barrier and tumbling over the embankment. Sienna and Parker both screamed, holding their hands on the roof of the car, as it rolled down the side and crashed upside down at the bottom of the hill.

Sienna could still hear the tires spinning as she came to. She wasn't sure how long she had been out for but it couldn't have been long. She looked over at Parker. She slapped his face and he startled awake.

"What happened?" he asked.

"We crashed." She kicked at her door until it creaked open. She crawled out onto the cold snow, her hands protesting against the frozen ground. She stood after her feet were outside the vehicle. She was brushing the snow off herself as Parker dragged himself out.

"Where are we?" he asked.

"No idea." She looked around and noticed a shack in the woods. "There! Let's go."

They trudged through the whipping snow to the shack. It was vacant and desolate but there was a fireplace and old wooden furniture.

"Here," Sienna said, handing Parker a lighter. "Break up one of those chairs and put it in the fireplace. Find some paper and light it. I'm going to see if I can get a signal on my phone."

"Why do I have to do it?"

"Parker, don't friggin' argue with me for once in your whole existence!" She shook her head and walked off toward the corner of the room. She tried to call 911 but her phone wasn't dialing out. She leaned her forehead against the cold glass, closing her eyes. Why her?

"We're going to have to wait until morning," she said, walking up to him. He was kicking at a second chair, a fire starting to crackle in the fireplace, cussing up a storm.

"Why?" he asked.

"I can't get a signal."

Parker stopped and turned to face her. "This is your fault."

"Excuse me?"

"You're the one who said we had to leave!"

"That was our original plan, Parker. We should have been done cleaning up over an hour before we were because there should have been two of us doing it. But no, somebody had to go take a nap instead."

"Oh, you're blaming this on me? Are you kidding me?"

"Yeah, I'm blaming it on you. I'm blaming this whole disaster on you. You're the little snot-nosed brat who didn't do jack shit today but yet still thinks it's acceptable to whine and cry and boohoo about how much this situation sucks and blame it all on me. Well, maybe next time, don't get your license revoked and you can make your own decisions."

"Such a bitch!"

Sienna slapped him across the face. He blinked, his mouth falling open, just gaping at her. "I am...so sick and tired of your attitude!"

"So you've said."

"I mean it." Sienna started pacing around the room. "I have put up with your shit for the past three months. But I am done!" She swung around to face him. She pointed at the chair. "Break the damn thing down and keep the fire going! I'm going to see if there's anything to eat." She stormed off into the kitchen, leaving him standing there in shock.

There were some cans of soup in the cupboards that weren't expired yet, but that would require wood for the woodstove. She walked out into the living room, where Parker was standing next to the fireplace, warming his hands. "Finish breaking up that chair. I need some wood for the stove."

"What? No."

"Yes. Do you want to eat?"

"I already ate. It's not my fault you didn't eat anything."

"I didn't eat anything because I was busy doing our job."

"Sucks to be you!"

His back was turned to her as he leaned over, warming his hands, and it was just too tempting and too inviting. Sienna hauled off and smacked him as hard as she could square on the ass. He yelped, jumped, and turned around to face her, his mouth agape.

"What was that for?" he asked, rubbing his seat like a four-year-old.

"That was for being a smart ass little shit. I have had it up to here with you, Parker Kensington. You're a spoiled rotten little brat whose parents give him everything he desires, including an internship that he does not deserve! I'm tired of catering to your every whim, listening to your whining, putting up with your bratty comments...I am completely and utterly done!"

Parker blinked a few times. "So, what, you're going to spank me?" he asked dryly.

Sienna crossed her arms. "I think that sounds like a fabulous idea."

His smug expression instantly left his face. "What?"

"That's the best idea I have ever heard you come up with."

"I'm not – I'm not just going to let you spank me!" he sputtered. "Are you out of your mind?"

"Oh, I think you will."

"Really? And why is that?"

"Because either you do or I will tell your parents that you nearly ruined this fundraiser. I will tell them that you didn't lift a finger to help. And above all, I will tell them that you were rude to their biggest benefactor. After already losing your license on their insurance, how fast do you think they'll take you off the internship? Hell, they might even yank your credit card and freeze your trust fund!"

"You wouldn't do that."

"Try me."

Parker stood there, just staring at her, and she could tell he was mulling it over in his mind.

"Think about it for a minute. I'll be right back." Sienna walked into the kitchen, trying to keep the bounce out of her step. She had dabbled in S&M with an ex-boyfriend, but she hadn't played in quite some time. The idea of beating Parker's ass made her giggle inside. She nabbed the rope in the corner of the room she had noticed earlier and sauntered out into the living room.

Parker's eyes got wide as he saw the rope.

"So what did you decide?" she asked.

"You know what I decided."

"Yes, but I want to hear you say it."

"Fine..." He hesitated and then said, "You can spank me."

"Good. Strip down to your boxers."

"What?" Parker asked.

"I said strip, Parker. Now!"

"Why?"

"From here until I say so, I'm the one in control," Sienna said. "So don't ask questions. Take off your shirt and your pants."

Parker swallowed hard. He slowly unbuttoned his shirt and tossed it onto the table. He pulled the undershirt off and added it to the pile.

Sienna watched as he took off his shoes. He had a nice upper body. His shoulders were thick and chiseled and his chest was tight. His stomach was a little soft around the midsection, but he obviously worked out now and then. It was hard to believe given how lazy he was. He laid his jeans on top of his shirts and turned to face her, standing in nothing but white briefs.

"Took you for a boxer kind of guy," she mused.

He said nothing.

"Nervous?" she asked.

"No," he lied.

She handed him an end of the rope. "Toss it over the rafters above you."

It took him a few tries but he got it over. She took the end that was dangling down. She placed his hands together in a praying position and wrapped the rope around his wrists, securing it tightly but without cutting off his circulation.

"Lean your elbows against the table," she told him.

Parker did as he was told. Sienna adjusted the slack and then tied part of the rope to a hanging pipe, making it impossible for Parker to go more than a foot away from where he was.

Sienna's eyes fell upon his backside. His briefs molded perfectly to his bubble butt. It was a cute butt and it suited him. She rested her left hand on his back, pressing down so he straightened it, sticking his ass out further. She pulled her right hand back and brought it down with a sharp crack against his cheek. He sucked in air but made no sounds. Sienna was going to make sure that changed by the end of the night. She quickly warmed his backside with her hand, landing crisp, swift spanks in a circular pattern all around, covering every square inch of his ass. It didn't take long before Parker was dancing around, yelping out, trying to get away from the onslaught.

"Ow! I get it, okay? Ow! I was a jerk! Ow! Stop!"

Sienna stopped for a moment and looked over at him. "You weren't just a jerk, Parker. You were a grade-A brat. If you don't want to get treated like a child, maybe you shouldn't act like one."

"It hurts, okay?"

"It's supposed to hurt. That's why it's a punishment." She reached into the hem of his briefs and yanked them down to his knees. The bright red color of his skin made her unable to keep from reaching out and touching it, rubbing her hand across the warmth. Parker let out a soft sigh. She watched goose flesh rise along his back.

"You need a serious attitude adjustment, Parker," Sienna told him, her hand still massaging his tender flesh. "Do you understand that?"

"Yeah."

She smacked his ass and he yelped. "You'll answer with 'yes, ma'am,' is that understood?"

"Yes, ma'am."

She tilted her head to the side, squinting curiously as he parted his legs while she rubbed his backside. The dangling jewels between them were too tantalizing. She allowed her hand to slide down and caress them, cupping them firmly. Parker let out a tiny groan.

She walked out into the kitchen and poked around for a bit until she found the proper tool. She picked the wooden spoon up and tested it against her hand. Nice and stingy. Should get the point across. She walked back into the room and was happy to see Parker still obediently bent over. Maybe there was hope for him yet.

Sienna wrapped her left arm around his waist and tapped the wooden spoon against his backside.

"Oh, come on! Please don't," he said.

"Just suck it up and take it like a man, Parker." And with that, she began to paddle him with the spoon, as hard and fast as she had with her hand. Each crack of the spoon was loud and echoing in the tiny empty cabin. His howls of pain were even louder. He squirmed all over, nearly knocking them to the ground a few times, but she held on tightly and didn't stop. Seeing he wasn't going anywhere, he bounced up and down on his feet and tried to move his butt away from the barrage of swats, yelping and begging her to stop.

"Please! I'm sorry! I'll never call you a bitch again! I'll never be rude again! I'll never be lazy again! I swear! Just please stop!" he whimpered, sounding close to tears.

Sienna stopped, having some mercy on him. He breathed heavily, his muscles relaxing underneath her arm. She examined her handiwork. She didn't expect any bruising, but it was pretty damn red, and she suspected he'd feel it for a day or two. She sat the spoon on the table and ran her hand across the abused flesh. Parker exhaled deeply, relaxing even more under her touch.

"I'm going to hold you to those promises, Parker," Sienna said.

"I know."

Her touch turned from tender to sensual, rubbing down his thighs and back up to his bum. Her body was thrumming. Her heart was pounding in her chest and she was dripping wet, soaking through her panties. The rush of power she'd gotten dominating Parker was making her ache for release. She slid her hand between his legs, wrapping it around his half-mast dick. Parker let out a tiny groan.

Sienna pulled on the rope and he stood, having no choice. She secured the rope so he couldn't move. Slowly, she stripped off her clothing. First, the blazer, then her blouse, then her pantyhose...she kept her eyes locked on Parker's as each article came off and fell to the floor. He licked his lips, watching her intently.

When she was standing in front of him naked, her eyes wandered down to his now rock hard erection. She stepped forward, giving him some slack.

"Down on your knees," she told him.

Parker obediently did as he was told. She placed her breast in his face and said, "Suck it."

He eagerly took the nipple into his mouth, flicking his tongue across the nub, raking his teeth against it, and suckling.

Sienna dug her nails into his shoulder, her other hand gripping his hair so he couldn't move his head. Heat flashed through her as his mouth worked fervently against her breast, first the left and then the right after she moved him. He was good with his tongue. So much so, Sienna wasn't about to stop here.

She hoisted herself up onto the table and beckoned him with the crook of her finger. He came to her and allowed his head to be placed between her legs. He needed no more invitation than that. He licked at her clit, sending a shot of liquid fire straight through her, a deep moan escaping from her throat. He flicked the sensitive bud back and forth with his tongue and Sienna gasped, gripping the edge of the table, shuddering as the first wave broke over her. She could take no more.

She yanked at the rope, giving him almost all the slack. She pushed him down onto the rug in front of the fireplace, settling herself onto him, burying his throbbing dick deep inside her. They both groaned in unison at the feeling. Sienna leaned back, rocking her hips against him, her nails digging into his thighs. Parker grunted and growled, thrusting his pelvis up to meet her. She leaned down, kissing him deeply, drinking in each rolling tide, each ebb and swell of pleasure.

Sienna sat up, twisting her hips, grinding against him. Parker closed his eyes and groaned.

"I think maybe a tiny part of you needs to admit that you enjoyed that a little," she remarked.

"And I think a tiny part of you needs to admit that you've been wanting to do this since we met."

She slapped his face, lightly but hard enough to sting, cause a tiny growl to rumble through his chest and his eyes to fly open, deep sapphire, and filled with desire.

Parker slung his still bound arms around her, pulling her forward, rising up, and plunging every inch of him inside of her. She let out a grunt of pleasure, scratching at his chest, trembling with the sensation.

Parker sat up, holding her rear, thrusting up into her, hitting just the right spots.

Sienna's nails sank into his shoulder and she threw her head back, screaming out, "Oh Parker!"

As she tightened around him in an explosive orgasm, he let out a deep groan and emptied his cream inside her.

They lay on the rug, panting heavily, the fire crackling in their ear and the ropes burning against Parker's wrists.

"Wow," he said. "That was one hell of a

punishment."
    "Same time tomorrow?"
    "Works for me."

AUTHOR'S NOTE

Readers: I want to expand a few of the stories to see where the characters can be explored further. If there are any of the stories that you would like to read more about again, I'd love to hear from you!

Visit my blog at
http://www.nicholerogue.com/

Join my newsletter for free exclusive previews
http://www.nicolerogue.com/in

Follow me on Twitter at
http://www.twitter.com/nicholerogue

Like my page on Facebook at
http://www.facebook.com/nicholerogue

Discover my books at major ebook retailers everywhere.

www.ingramcontent.com/pod-product-compliance
Lightning Source LLC
Chambersburg PA
CBHW032018170626
46807CB00006B/2862